The Romanov Star

A novel

Dan Goldstein

Dan Goldstein

ISBN No. 978- 0- 9889253-5-9 (print edition)

Disclaimer

This book is a work of fiction and is intended for the reader's enjoyment only. Names, characters, places and incidents are either the product of the author's imagination or are used fictitiously. Any resemblance to actual events or locales or persons, living or dead, is coincidental.

Dan Goldstein

TABLE OF CONTENTS

Chapter One

Justin Wade, private investigator, was sitting at his desk staring into space, wondering when his next case was going to walk through the door, when she entered. She took two steps into the large, dark, mahogany covered room with a look of disapproval on her face. He saw her eyes scan the dimly lit office, hesitating for an instant as she looked through the open door to the bathroom.

Justin could see the disgusted look on her face; as though she made a mistake, and wanted to retrace her steps. Then her eyes focused on him.

His hands, which were holding up his head, came down from his cheeks.

"You're Justin Wade," she said with disdain.

Was that a question or a statement? "Yeah, Wade. That's me. What's the matter? You don't like the looks of my office?" He sneered at her.

"It's a dump," she shot back at him.

"Nobody forced you into this dump," he volleyed back at her.

"You're right. I was told you're the best private detective in town."

He snorted. "Maybe because I'm the only private detective in town."

"No matter." She waved a perfectly manicured hand. "I need some help. And you look scroungy enough to get yourself dirty helping me."

"Oh. Is that so? Do I look that scroungy?" He rose from behind his large wooden desk and looked down at his un-pressed pants and stocking feet.

"Well," she answered. "You're not dressed at the height of fashion, but what can anybody expect from a private detective?"

She was beginning to piss him off. "Listen, lady." He tucked his shirt into his pants and pulled at his crotch. "If you don't like what you see, the door is still open behind you."

"I need you," she said with reservation.

He openly eyed her up and down. Her long, black, coiffured hair framed the olive colored skin of her face. What a knock-out body under her black and white herringbone skirt. Her breasts bulged from under the double breasted, matching suit jacket. Her legs were about as shapely as any he had ever seen. Expensive clothes, designer bag, rocks on her fingers that looked real. He paused long enough to enjoy the deep cleavage between her round full breasts. "Well, I could use you too, but we hardly know each other," he snickered with a half-smile cutting across his face.

A rose tinge crept up from that glorious cleavage, up her neck and onto her high cheekbones. She brought his mind back to reality when she said, "Are you through?"

"Huh? Oh, I'm sorry. It isn't every day that a woman as beautiful as you walks through my door.

"You're a wise guy, aren't you? And very rude, I might add."

"Wise enough to know who I want to work for," he answered. "What's your name?"

"It's Berns, Susan Berns. May I sit?"

Justin gestured toward a chair, then realized it was covered in old newspapers. He quickly brushed them off on to the floor. "Berns, huh?"

"Berns is my married name. Look, can we get down to business? Do you want my business, or don't you?"

"Depends, what exactly do you need me to do?"

"I need you to find my husband."

Justin dropped back into his chair behind his desk. "Your husband? Did he run off with a little twenty-something?"

"Yes, and no, he did not run off with a twenty-something, but there are also my missing jewels. I need you to find those, especially, one very old and expensive necklace. It's a family heirloom."

He shook his head. Some broads are so dumb. "Jesus, isn't it obvious that if your husband is missing and your jewels are gone, he took them and skipped?"

Her eyes blazed at him. "No. It's not obvious. He's not the type to do something like that. Besides, he doesn't need my jewels."

"What else can you tell me? Has he been acting strange? Are you sure he's wasn't diddling your maid? I assume you do have a maid, don't you?"

"Of course I have a maid. Doesn't everybody?" For the first time, she smiled.

She was really quite exquisite when she smiled. Not a flaw on her smooth face.

"Hell, if your husband has skipped out on you, he's one major fool. I'd lock you in the bedroom and throw away the key."

"Mr. Wade. If you locked me in the bedroom, I would jump out the window . . . and my bedroom is on the second floor."

"I see that you like me," he answered as a grin spread across his face.

"Sure, okay. Do you have a picture of your husband? I could use a description of the missing jewelry also."

"I have both right here." She rummaged through her matching black and white bag.

"My husband's name is Sterling Berns . . . from Boston." She walked toward his desk and held out two pictures, a list of the missing jewelry, the necklace and a business card.

"Boston huh? I'm from Revere, right outside of Boston."

She didn't respond.

Justin took the pictures from her slowly, their hands briefly touching. Setting the photos on the desk without looking at them, their eyes met and held. He could feel her stare burn through him and tap into his soul.

Thank God for the desk between them. He could barely hold himself back from grabbing her and planting a sloppy kiss on her perfect, beautiful lips.

She broke away from the meeting of their eyes and said, "Don't be getting rambunctious now. Maybe if you were my type . . ."

That broke the spell. "What the hell do you mean by that —your type?"

"Well, let's face it, Mr. Wade. You're not the cleanest looking guy I've seen today."

"Look, Mrs. Berns. I just came off a thirty-eight hours stake-out. Just how pretty do you think you'd be after thirty-eight hours crammed in a car?

Susan Berns nodded. "Well, maybe next time we see each other you'll look more like a human being."

Justin said, "Maybe next time you see me you'll be looking up at me, or down . . . whichever meets your fancy."

She stretched her long legs and stood. "Well, Mr. Wade, if I were you, I wouldn't hold my breath."

He stared at her for a moment, thinking about how he'd like to see her below him, holding her breath. The thought made him shudder with longing. He wasn't ready for her to leave. He picked up the photo on the desk. Mr. Berns was handsome, in a too-perfect way. Perfectly groomed, Armani suit, Hermes tie. His brown hair was styled, not a hair out of place. In comparison, Justin looked crude. His dark, Romanian skin seemed in start contract to the faire skinned Sterling Berns. Berns looked serious, not the kind that knew how to have a good time. *Some people say I have boyish good looks*, thought Justin. Of course, some of those were hookers.

"What else can you tell me about your husband?" he asked, breaking away from his comparison of himself and her husband.

She sat back down. "He left for New York six nights ago. He called me from there when he landed, and the following two nights, before he went to sleep. There was no reason that he shouldn't have returned by now. I called the hotel. They told me he'd checked out three days ago. As far as they remember, he mentioned that he would be catching a plane back to Boston that same evening."

"To Boston," he repeated her. "What the hell are you talking about? What are you doing in Florida when you're expecting him back in Boston?"

Susan Berns fidgeted with the clasp on her bag. "Sterling was to come back to Boston, that's right. After he hadn't arrived, I went through some of his papers and found an address and phone number of a Rochelle Gauvin, here in Naples. That's her phone number that I gave you," she said pointing toward the pictures and papers she had set on the desk.

"I tried to reach her for an entire day but she wouldn't take my calls. It made me suspicious. So I decided to come to Florida in person. For some reason she's been avoiding me. I only realized the jewels were missing when I packed to fly down here."

"Well," Justin said. "I'm the only P I in Naples, so you don't have much choice. The police won't help you in a case like this."

"I know that, Mr. Wade. I asked around. The sergeant at the front desk of the police station suggested I contact you."

"You must mean Sergeant Toody Muldoon."

That beautiful smile again. "Toody? Did you say Toody Muldoon?"

"That's not his real name. We're good friends and we joke about his name. His real name is John Muldoon. Toody Muldoon used to be a character in a comic show on television, years ago."

"I know that. I remember seeing it a few times. That's why I questioned it."

Their eyes met. "Anyway, Mrs. Berns. Where are you staying?"

"You can reach me at the Ritz Carlton."

Of course. Where else would a classy lady like this stay? "Need I have asked?"

A corner of her perfect mouth turned up. "Maybe if you cleaned up, I could let you buy me a drink this evening."

"Maybe I'll let you buy me a drink."

"That depends, Mr. Wade." She hesitated. "May I ask what sort of case you just finished? Or, are you finished?"

"I'm through with that. Case solved. Nothing spectacular. A wayward wife. She was screwing the entire town. Her husband thought she had one boyfriend. Turns out, she had a different one every night. As you probably know, there's many retirees here in Naples. Some of them are pretty well loaded. This guy didn't want to leave his money to a run around wife, so he hired me to find out what she's been up to."

"How old are they," she asked.

Justin laughed out loud. "That's the funny part. He's eighty-one and she's seventy-two."

She matched his laugh. "And she's running around?"

"Yeah, and she doesn't look a day over sixty. All her lovers were in their fifties and sixties. Hard to believe, huh? She's one horny old broad."

Susan Berns' face flushed. "My goodness, she must be. May I ask, how old are you?"

She really knew how to surprise him. "I thought it was impolite to ask a person's age. Oh yea, that's a woman's age. How old do you want me to be?"

"Maybe forty . . . forty-five."

"That's funny. I'm forty-three."

"That's a fine age, Mr. Wade" she whispered.

Justin stood and walked around the desk, close to Mrs. Berns. "Tell me something, Mrs. Berns. Are you looking for your husband simply to find the jewels, or is it because you love him?"

"I want my jewel's back, and naturally I want him to be okay. As of the day he left for New York, I was still the heir to his fortune. But as far as loving him . . . that ended many years ago. We sort of tolerate each other now. But I certainly don't want anything bad to happen to him. That's why I'm asking you to find him. I'll be honest with you. I fear that something bad has already happened. Otherwise he would've been in touch with me by now."

"Okay, Mrs. Berns. Maybe I'll see you tonight."

"I have dinner at eight," she said, standing to leave. "That's eight sharp! If you're not there on time, don't bother coming."

"Don't bother coming, huh? I'd better not touch that, Mrs. Berns."

"No. I don't think you should." She spun around and walked out the door.

Justin sat heavily into his swivel chair, his exhaustion about to overcome him. He swung around looking side to side, taking in the squalor of his surroundings. The once white window shades were now a dull yellow, faded by the heavy-duty sunshine of southwest Florida. The rug was worn thin in several places. The bit of wallpaper near the ceiling was peeling away from the wall, like a small wave frozen in time. He felt safe here, in his office. But he knew that's not what makes a good detective.

Why hadn't he noticed how terrible this place looked before? He mumbled to himself, "This place is a dump." Maybe if he solved the beautiful lady's problem, he could squeeze enough money to get a better office place. At least it had a shower and room to crash if he didn't feel like going home to his condo. It was then that he realized . . . "Son-of-a-bitch," he said aloud. "I never gave her my rates." Well, there was always tonight.

What could he expect from his dinner with Susan Berns tonight? It felt like there was spark, but it was filtered with sarcasm and condescension. She was definitely hot. Didn't she say she wasn't in love with her husband anymore? He could have a shot, right? Who was he kidding? She was way out of his league.

Damn. He never explained that the stake-out required that he look "scroungy" as she called it. She probably thought he looked like that all the time. And his office didn't do anything to give him any other opinion. Well, he'd surprise her tonight. He could clean up real good. He leaned back in his chair, his eyes closed and he drifted into a deep sleep.

Chapter Two

The police sirens woke Justin with a start. He looked at the old, wood clock on the wall and saw it was early afternoon. He locked the door to the office and stripped away his dirty, wrinkled clothes. He walked to the open bathroom door and stepped through it. Under the spigot was a trail of rust from the continual dripping water. The lone window, half hidden behind the yellowed white window shade, hadn't been cleaned in years. The wall paper had been painted over years ago. Now a faded grey, he wondered why it wasn't blue like he remembered it. He reached in and turned the hot water spigot on. It took over a minute for the hot water to reach his shower head. He surveyed his naked body in the cracked mirror. He sucked in his gut. Perhaps time to take back up jogging. Damn, he hated jogging. When the steam started to fill the rusty shower stall, he took a long hot shower.

Justin pulled the black double breasted suit he had purchased two weeks earlier from the lone hook on the wall. He forgot to bring fresh boxers from home. He checked. No skid marks and put yesterday's back on. The only tie at the office was ice blue and white. His last girlfriend had given it to him. Not Hermes, but a nice match. He dressed and admired himself in the long mirror.

"Not bad, not bad at all, Justin Wade. You're okay," he said aloud. At his desk, he put through a call to the number Mrs. Berns had given him.

"Bruce Travel Agency," a male voice answered.

"May I please speak with Rochelle Gauvin?"

"I'm sorry. Mrs. Gauvin is out of the office. May I help you? This is Richard Gauvin, her husband."

"Do you own the agency, Mr. Gauvin?"

"Yes. My wife and I own it together. The Bruces' were the former owners. We decided not to change the name. May I help you?"

"Maybe. Does the name Sterling Berns mean anything to you?"

"Uh, oh, ah, no. I don't know any Sterling Berns. Please, I'm very busy. I'm not able to answer any questions." The line went dead.

Justin looked at the receiver in his hand. Why did Gauvin sound so afraid?

His second call was to his friend, Robert McNally, a local Realtor®. Robert was a little light in the loafers, but he was a good agent and knew Collier County like the back of his hand.

"Robert, you've got to find me a better place. This place is a hell hole." They talked about areas, prices and square footage requirements. An adjoining bath with a shower was a must.

As Justin entered the dining room of the plush, Ritz Carlton Hotel, he couldn't help but notice the sea of grey hair. Almost everybody eating dinner was in their golden years. Mrs. Berns' beauty stood out like a rose in a thistle garden. Her dark hair cascaded softly around her face. The simple little black dress with a double strand of white pearls around her slender neck, the matching pearl ear rings, everything was exquisite and complimented her beautiful olive colored skin.

Every man in the place was stealing looks at her every chance they had. Justin nodded to her as he approached her table. He understood why all the old men couldn't stop looking at her. She was quite beautiful.

"Good evening Mrs. Berns," he said.

"Pardon me," she replied, barely looking up from her martini. "Have we met?"

She was serious. She didn't recognize him. Was that a compliment or an insult? Justin wasn't sure. He'd take the defensive.

"Of course we've met . . . just hours ago. Does my putting on decent clothes change my appearance that much?"

She looked up and their eyes met. "I beg your pardon . . . oh, I'm terribly sorry, Mr. Wade. My God, you look so different."

Justin felt a grin spread across his face, trying to straighten his already straight tie. "For the better I hope."

Her eyes twinkled. "Oh my, yes. You look absolutely . . . nice."

Justin smiled to himself. Was she about to say absolutely good enough to eat? *Wishful thinking, Wade ole' boy. Get your mind out of the gutter.*

"Thank you. I must say you don't look so bad yourself."

"Mr. Wade. I don't think you phrased that quite well. Was that supposed to be a compliment?"

"My apologies. Let me rephrase it this way. You look scrumptious, Mrs. Berns. Good enough to eat." A man's got to try, right?

She didn't even flinch. "Why, thank you, Mr. Wade. How you do go on," she tittered in her best Southern bell drawl. She was toying with him.

"May I sit?" Justin asked.

"Of course, Mr. Wade."

"Please, call me Justin, and may I call you, Susan?" he asked.

"Do you really think that's advisable?"

"Definitely. If we became friends I might put more of my heart and soul into this investigation. Especially since I have an ulterior motive."

"Oh?"

Justin sipped at his glass of water. Where was the waiter? A swanky place like that should have waiters crawling up your ass. He needed a drink. "Yes, I really hope to find out that your husband ran off with another woman."

"That's a terrible thing to say. Why would you want that?"

A waiter appeared and interrupted their conversation. He took Justin's drink order and Justin continued. "That way I would have a clear field."

"A clear field for what?" Her eyes were glued on his.

"I think you know what I mean, Susan."

A pink glow colored her cheeks. "Yes, I suppose I do. Have you done anything about my case yet, Justin?" She abruptly changed the subject.

"Just a call to that telephone number you gave me. I spoke with Richard Gauvin. He was very abrupt and seemed rattled when I mentioned your husband's name. I intend to follow up with a visit in the morning."

"May I go with you?"

"I don't think so. I prefer to work alone. Not that I wouldn't want you around, but there's no telling what path any of this may take and I don't want to endanger you in any way."

"You're looking out for my welfare. That's nice," she whispered.

He stared into her eyes. Dark hair and blue eyes, the sign of a beautiful woman. The longer he looked at her the more lovely she became. He found it hard to break from her spell.

Was it possible that Susan was attracted to him also, or was that only wishful thinking?

"Justin, let's order." She leaned over the table and quietly said, "This is too fast. I just met you. I'm married and I have some important matters to attend to. Please understand."

"Of course, Susan. I'll solve this mystery soon, then maybe there will be time for us."

"Perhaps," she responded.

They had dinner and a liqueur. He relaxed and began to tell her about himself. He'd never done that before. He kept things close to the vest. Now he couldn't seem to stop talking. What kind of magic did she have over him?

"I'm a veteran of the Viet Nam War. I was a cop in a small town outside of Boston. A town called Revere. When I was discharged from the Marines I decided I wanted to be a cop, so I became one of Revere's finest. I worked my way up to detective and was doing fine until I ran into a new police chief. We didn't see eye to eye so I quit and came to Florida. I considered becoming a cop down here but after thinking about it for a while, I decided to go out on my own. I've never been married." He suddenly stopped, aware of how he was rambling. He took a long gulp of his Scotch and water, "Is there anything more you want to know about me?"

"I didn't ask for any of that," she said, "but I appreciate your candor."

When it was time to leave she excused herself, kissed him on the cheek, and left him standing beside the table watching her leave. Being a leg man, he was in awe of what was walking away from him. Every man in the room enjoyed her exit as well. Yes, you grey-haired ass-holes. That was me she just kissed on the cheek.

He looked at the bill and about choked. Did he have that much available cash on his credit card? If he was going to entertain women like this, he'd better raise his rates.

After breathing a sigh of relief when the card when through, he called his friend, Sergeant John Muldoon from his cell phone in the lobby.

"Toody, listen. I need some info on a couple here in Naples. Rochelle and Richard Gauvin. They own and run the Bruce Travel Agency. Okay, pal?"

"Okay, Justin," John answered. "Check back with me in about an hour. Hey, listen. Dorothy's been on my back about having a cook-out this Sunday. She wants to get all our friends together, can you make it?"

"Sure. Tell her I can hardly wait to see her pretty face again. And if it's okay with you, I might bring a woman friend."

"A woman friend? You have a friend?" John choked into the phone. Very funny. "By all means, bring your friend. If she's willing to go out with you more than once, she must be something. I bet she's a hooker . . . or a dog . . . but bring her anyway."

"She is not a hooker, or a dog. Toody . . . you just hold onto your socks cause she's gonna' blow them off."

When he gets a look at Susan, if she'll even go, well, it'll blow his mind.

John laughed and said, "Okay, Justin. Get back to me in an hour. If I'm out for any reason, I'll end up at Bad Boy's Restaurant. Meet me there for coffee."

"Got it, Toody. Later."

Justin drove to his place at the Foxfire condo development, undressed and quickly slipped between the sheets and within minutes was in a deep sleep.

He awakened with a start. "Damn," he said aloud. He only meant to close his eyes for a little bit. He reached for the phone and punched in the numbers for Bad Boy's Restaurant.

"Hi, Ray, Wade here. Is Sergeant Muldoon still there?" A few moments passed as Justin listened to the glasses clanging, servers barking orders to the cook, and mumbled voices of restaurant patrons.

"Sergeant Muldoon here."

"Toody, sorry pal, I fell asleep. What can you tell me?"

"It seems your Gauvin couple are a couple of scam artists. There are loads of complaints from customers. What's going on, Justin?"

"I have a missing person, John. I'm not sure these people are involved, yet. But the husband seemed nervous when I asked about the MP. If I need your help, I'll be in touch. I'd come up there but I'm totally exhausted. I'll catch you tomorrow, either at the station or at home. Oh, and tell Dorothy I can't wait until I can kiss her hello again."

"Okay Slick, I know she'll be happy that you're coming. Just make sure when you get there, you keep your hands to yourself."

"Hell, Toody, you know I can't keep my hands off your wife, but I will have my own squeeze this time." That was, if Susan agreed to go with him.

"Yea, right," John said with a smile in his voice. "Catch you tomorrow."

Justin reached for the slip of paper with the number of the Ritz Carlton, punched the numbers into his phone and asked for Susan's room.

"Hello?" Her voice purred through the phone.

"I hope I didn't wake you. It's Justin. I was laying here and couldn't get your face out of my mind. I hope you don't mind my calling."

"No, I don't mind. Actually, I thought I'd hear from you earlier. What took you so long?"

"I was busy checking out some thoughts I have on Rochelle Gauvin. I'm not sure yet, but there's a chance that they're involved in something. I don't want to tell you anything until I know some truths. But I'm getting away from the reason I called."

Before he had a chance to say anything further, she interrupted him. "What was your reason, Justin?" Her voice sounded teasing. Was she playing with him?

"I thought . . . uh, well, I guess it's really too late now . . . look, Susan." He felt his temples pounding in his head. "I've been invited to a cook-out to go to this Saturday. My friend, Toody Muldoon invited me and I said yes I would go. I don't suppose you'd like to go with me."

"Of course, I'd love to go with you," she answered in a whisper.

Just like that, she took the wind out of his sales. Should he tell her what else he hand in mind?

"I was hoping you might ask me to come back to the hotel tonight."

She had a low, sexy guttural laugh. "Were you? Well, a couple of hours ago I might have said yes. Now, it's too late. I'm very tired."

His disappointment was palatable.

"Besides," she continued. "If you only wanted to come here for a booty call, you could have gone downtown and got some company."

Now that was unfair. He felt anger spur in his gut. "Wait a minute, Susan. I just wanted to see you again. Jesus Christ, do you really think so little of me?" The fact that he was hoping for some action was beside the point.

She sighed into the phone. "Justin, cool down. Call me when you have something to tell me about my husband. I'll be around the hotel somewhere. Have them page me if I'm not in my room."

Justin didn't want to cool down. "Look, Susan, we never discussed my fee."

She burst out laughing. "Your fee? We don't have to discuss it. You won't cheat me and whatever you charge, I can pay. "

"Right," Justin said as he hung up the phone, mumbling under his breath . . . "Bitch!"

Justin's alarm clock went off at seven a.m. Damn it. Where did the night go? He slowly removed himself from his 70's water bed and walked slowly into the large tiled shower stall. He loved his shower, with all the room it provided for which ever lady he was seeing at the time. There was enough room to actually lay down in a sexual embrace, and it was in much better shape than the scroungy – her word – one at the office.

Justin dressed in a worn pair of white chinos, a light blue T-shirt and a dark blue sport jacket. Very Miami Vice. He slid behind the wheel of his 1982 El

Dorado Cadillac. Was he stuck in the past? Perhaps, but he loved the Caddy, so much so he had a new engine installed when the speedometer reached one-hundred and forty thousand miles. A month after that he replaced the transmission. The Caddy was a sharp car with the Rolls-Royce grill and a false Continental tire at the rear. He always referred to it as his 'pimp mobile'.

The Bruce Travel Agency was near downtown. Tourist season made the traffic terrible, especially on the Tamiami Trail, otherwise known as U.S. Route 41. As he pulled around the back of the building, he saw two big Buicks parked side by side. He noticed the license plates. One plate had the letters BTA-1, the other was BTA-2. The letters must stand for Bruce Travel Agency. If so, it meant that both husband and wife were there. He parked his Caddy and walked through the front door.

"I'd like to speak with Rochelle Gauvin," he said to a young receptionist chomping on her gum.

A voice carried from an open door to a private office, "I'm Rochelle Gauvin. May I help you?

Justin walked through the door to see a plain looking, middle-aged, dark-haired woman standing just inside the door.

"Whom am I talking to?" she asked.

"My name is Justin Wade. I represent Susan Berns. I talked to your husband yesterday. I asked him if he knew Sterling Berns. He lied to me when he said he didn't know him."

"No, Mr. Wade. He didn't lie to you. He doesn't know Mr. Berns. But I do know that name. He spoke with me on the phone a few nights ago from Boston. He was looking into a flight down here, to Naples. I received that call, then I never heard from him again. There's nothing else I can tell you."

She had to be lying. Why else would her husband sound so nervous on the phone if they didn't know him?

"May I speak with your husband?" Justin asked.

"Of course, be my guest."

Justin walked over to Richard Gauvin sitting behind his desk, shuffling papers. "Mr. Gauvin. My name is Justin Wade. I spoke to you yesterday on the phone. I represent Susan Berns. I'm trying to locate her husband, Sterling Berns. Is there anything you can tell me?"

The sweat on Gauvin's top lip told Justin many things; mainly that this man was scared out of his skin.

"I told you on the phone. I don't know anything about a Sterling Berns. Why don't you leave us alone?"

"I'm only looking for leads, Mr. Gauvin. Nobody's accusing you of anything. I'm only trying to locate him. Your wife said she spoke to him on the phone. Did you talk to him as well?"

"Yes, no, I mean no, I didn't talk to him. Only my wife talked to him, not me. I can't tell you a thing. Look, I'm quite busy. If that's all, would you please leave me alone so I can go back to work? We have a business to run."

Justin raised his hands in a motion of surrender. "Sorry. I didn't mean to cause you any trouble." Justin walked from the agency and drove directly to the Ritz Carlton.

Chapter Three

As he walked into the Ritz Carlton lobby he heard his name called. He turned to see Susan reading tourist pamphlets.

"Good morning, Justin," she said as he approached.

"Good morning, Susan. I'd like to go over the list of stolen jewelry with you. I took a glance at it but I believe I need a better description of some items. Where would you like to do this?"

"We could sit in the lounge." She smiled. There it was . . . the smile that turned his gut into mush.

"Wouldn't you be more comfortable in your room?" He flashed her is best smile.

Just as quickly, her smile vanished. "We both have a job to do and I don't want to lose focus on why I'm here. My job is to supply you with all the information I can. Your job is to find Sterling, and the jewelry."

"I see. Okay, let's get to it." Was his disappointment visible? He must stay aloof. What did he care if she shut him down? She was just a client.

"I need some sketches or photos of the stolen items."

"I'm not an artist, Justin, nor do I have any photos. My insurance man has all of that. Nor can I remember all the details of all the items taken. Some of them are heirlooms and antiques and I'm sure I can't give you any details on those. All I know is some of them were very valuable and I want them back."

"Well, until I receive something from your insurance man, you'll have to do the best you can. Look, don't worry, I won't be making any passes at you."

"No? You mean I'm safe for a while?" Her lips turned in a slight smile.

This damn woman was going to give him blue balls. "As far as I'm concerned, you're safe forever. I don't like being made a fool of." Justin took her by the arm, not too tenderly, and led her toward the elevators. "Let's get this job done. What floor are you on?"

"Seven. Room seven-twelve." She placed her hand on his arm. "I didn't mean to make a fool of you, Justin. I'm sorry if that's how you took it."

He stopped short and spun her around to face him. "And as for my bathroom, its mine, not yours. You don't have to worry about using it, and that goes for my office too. So, don't be so God-damn critical. Let's get this damn job done." The minute the words were out of his mouth he regretted them. Where did that come from? Why would she even be thinking about his bathroom or office? Man, he was losing it around this woman.

Justin and Susan sat side-by-side on the living room sofa with sketches strewn all over the coffee table. She tried to sketch rings, ear rings bracelets and necklaces. "I'm not very good at this." She set down the sketch pad and pencil, clearly frustrated with her results.

"Let's work on one at a time. Perhaps the antique heirloom necklace, I have an idea." He reached for the phone and called down to the lobby, asking for the concierge.

"Good morning," Justin said. "I'm in need of a catalogue, preferably jewelry catalogues. Tiffany, Cartier, something like that."

"Certainly sir. To what room, sir?"

"Seven Twelve. Thank you." He turned to Susan. "Let's take a break until we hear from him. Maybe with luck that'll give us a start."

Susan leaned back and covered a yawn.

"Didn't you sleep well last night?" Justin asked.

"Actually, I slept quite well, probably too much. I don't know why I feel so tired."

Justin wanted to touch her cheek, but he refrained. "Maybe you were dreaming about me and it disturbed your sleep?"

"No, I don't think so. If I dreamed of you, that would have been a nightmare," she said with a coy smile.

Was she busting his balls again? Justin felt anger rise and then quickly subside when he saw the look on her face. He had to learn not to take her dry humor so seriously.

"I'm sorry, I didn't mean to say that, Justin. No, I didn't dream of you, but if I did it certainly wouldn't have been a nightmare. It's true. I am attracted to you but right now I have other things on my mind. If I intend to let you get to me I want to be able to give my whole self to you, not spread my feelings in too many directions."

"Well," Justin said. "At least were getting somewhere. A bit of honesty is all I was looking for. All I . . ."

Justin's words were cut short by a knock on the door. A bell boy handed Justin a thick catalogue and an envelope. He opened the envelope to read what the concierge had written.

"This is the best I could do at short notice. If you need something different, let me know." The note was signed: Mr. De Louise, Concierge.

"Well, pretty lady, this might just do it. I want you to scan through this catalog and pick out the jewelry that most resembles what was taken from you. Especially the necklace. I'll order up some coffee and snacks. Take your time, this could be very important."

Justin sat on the opposite side of the room munching on a sandwich and drinking coffee as Susan scrolled through the catalogue page by page. Justin was starting to doze when he heard her talking.

"There are so many things in here that look like things I had. But nothing that looks anything like my necklace." He watched her as she rose from the sofa and glided across the floor to the refrigerator in the corner of the room. He couldn't keep his eyes from locking onto her beautiful legs and shapely rear.

Susan caught him shaking his head from side to side. "You like what you see?" she asked.

"Yes, Susan, more than you know."

She returned to her sofa and continued scanning the pages, occasionally glancing up at Justin. He liked how she stared at him from time to time. Would she make a move? She had made it quite clear that she wanted to keep it strictly business for now.

He stared out the window at beautiful Naples beach. This is why he left Massachusetts, for the sun, the mild Gulf, the beautiful women with lots of skin showing.

"This is it! Justin, this is it. It looks exactly like my heirloom necklace. But this must be a copy. Mine's been passed down from generation to generation and is worth a lot of more than the three thousand price tag here." Her face suddenly lit up. "I remember now. It had a very important name. It's called the Romanov Star. It's been years since I've thought about that."

Justin stared at the picture. He knew he was no expert on jewelry, but this was so over the top that it was just plain ugly in his opinion. "You're right. I'm sure it's a copy. Susan, why didn't you have it copied yourself? Most insurance companies insist on it.

"My insurance man did suggest that, but we never got around to it. Somebody must have, perhaps by parents or grandparents. I didn't know it, if they did. How else could a replica end up here?"

Justin tore the page from the catalogue, neatly folded it and put it in his inside jacket pocket.

"Do you see any others that look familiar to the other stolen pieces?"

"I'll continue looking, but I've already folded back several pages where the item looks similar to mine. I'll continue to the end of the book."

Susan turned the last page, stood up and stretched. The buttons on her blouse came close to popping.

Justin's pants were suddenly tight as well. The sight brought a knowing smile to his lips. If he played his cards right, in time he'd be making love to that beautiful lady.

He watched her walk over to the coffee pot. It wasn't her body, as beautiful as it was. It was the way she carried herself. Regal, back straight and head held high. Was she taught to walk like that, or was she born with it? She was a lady from the tip of her toes to the top of her head. What a lucky bastard that Sterling Berns is. Why in God's name would he leave something like that? Even jewels wouldn't tempt him to leave her . . . if he ever had her.

He hated to end his time with her, but there was something he had to do.

"Susan," he said. "I have to take a quick ride to Miami. It's about a two-hour drive. I'll probably spend a couple of hours there so I might be back a bit late. I'll pick you up tomorrow morning about eleven in the morning for the cook-out. Is that okay?"

"Why are you going to Miami?" She handed him a cup of coffee, black, just like he liked it. "...if you don't mind my asking?"

"No, it makes no difference. I have to end something and I don't want to do it over the phone. That's not my style. I like to do things face to face."

She leaned over the coffee table, giving Justin a direct view down her blouse. "I'll bet you do, but there are other ways to do it, you know," she said seductively.

Was she implying what he thought she was implying? She ran so hot and cold. How was a man to keep up?

Keep it together Wade. "I know, but in this case I'm breaking off a relationship with a young lady. If you want to talk dirty with me, it'll have to wait for another day. I'll see you in the morning."

"Okay, Justin. Be a good boy while you're over there."

"We don't owe each other anything, Susan. Your business is yours and my business is mine."

She didn't answer. She stared into his eyes' until he broke his gaze away and walked out the door.

Justin spotted Susan the minute he walked into the lobby of the Ritz at exactly eleven o'clock in the morning. She was waiting for him, again. He liked that.

She stood and walked toward him, kissing him on the cheek as she whispered, "Good morning, Justin. I hope things went well for you last night."

Did she kiss everyone hello and goodbye? He hoped not, but he could get used to it. He reciprocated with a brush of a kiss on her perfect cheek. "Yes, things went fine. It was difficult, but I did what I had to do and drove right back. I was home in bed by midnight."

"Really?" She handed him his usual black coffee. "I thought you might have even stayed the night."

"No, Susan. When I end something, it's ended. It wasn't that I didn't care for her. I did. But long distance relationships weren't working for either of us. I called her one night and a man answered. That was the end of that, as far as I was concerned. She regretted the whole situation, but what the hell . . ." *And now there is you.*

"Are you ready to go to Toody's?" Susan asked, changing the subject.

"Yep, let's go. I think you're going to love his wife, Dorothy. She and I like to joke and tease each other. She's a real good sport. Her mother will be there along with some other cops and mutual friends. I met John through Dorothy's mother. She was raised in Russia and came to the States through Ellis Island."

"Really, how interesting," said Susan, tucking her arm in his as they left the hotel.

"Yep, they changed her name to O'Reilly because one of the Irish immigration cops took a liking to her. That was when they allowed some Jews to migrate out of Russia. Her real name is Ruth Oskivitz. That's also how I got my name—Wade. My mother came from a small village called Wadi in Russia. She overheard me talking in a store about Romania and Russia and stopped to talk to me. Once she learned that I was Jewish and Romanian, she sort of adopted me, like a surrogate mother." There he goes again, diarrhea of the mouth. Why does he do that around her?

"So you're Jewish?"

Ugh-oh. "Why, is that a problem?"

Susan squeezed his arm. "No silly. I'm just asking. Trying to understand the storyline. Go ahead. I didn't mean to interrupt."

"Well, she introduced me to Dorothy and through them, I met John. We got along so well we've become very good friends. He helps me often with my cases, things that can save me time to find out for myself. He's a really good cop."

"So, if I've got this straight. We are going to a picnic with your best friend and his wife's family. And they are like family to you? Did I get it all?"

Was she making fun of him again? He only wanted to fill her in on the situation. Justin turned to look at her and saw the slight smile across her lips. Damn, she got him again. He smiled and as they walked toward his car he banged his hip into hers and received her hip back in return. She smiled all the way to the car.

Justin and Susan walked around to the back of John and Dorothy's house and entered the yard through the large white gate. Justin immediately walked to Dorothy's mother, kissing her on the cheek.

"Mom, I want you to meet a special lady. This is Susan Berns. Susan, this is my adopted mom, Ruth O'Reilly."

The women hugged and made small talk as Justin stood aside enjoying the sight. They were hitting it off very well.

Justin took Susan by the arm and said, "Excuse

me, Mom. I want Susan to meet Dorothy and John. John seemed to think I would be bringing a dog with me. Now I want to see his socks blown off when he sees this lovely lady."

He and Susan approached John, standing behind his barbecue. When he saw the expression on John's face turn from blasé to one of astonishment, he whispered to Susan, "You just blew his socks off, Sweetie."

Susan smiled, looked at Justin. "Didn't I blow your socks off? I thought I did. If not, then I'll have to try harder."

Justin didn't have time to react to her remark when John shook his hand, standing back a moment before Justin introduced them.

"I believe we've already met." John said, taking her hand. "At the police station, correct?"

"Yes, that's right. You were the officer that recommended Justin as a P.I. to me." She beamed at Justin. "Thank you for that."

"Justin said he was going to bring a beautiful woman, but, I never thought he'd show up with the likes of you. You certainly do brighten up the party."

"I understand your wife is a very pretty lady," Susan said. "Where is she?"

John took her by the arm and walked her into the house to introduce her to his wife, leaving Justin standing by himself.

Mom appeared by his side, "Is she your new lady or is she just a date, Justin?"

"I don't know yet. Actually she's a client but I'd like to see it go further. Right now she's married, but her husband is missing. I have a gut feeling that he may be dead. I don't know what the story is just yet, but I believe he was into something crooked and didn't make it."

"A married woman with a missing husband? Be careful, Justin." She frowned and then turned her lips up into a smile. "But it would be nice seeing her again. She seems your type."

Justin gave his surrogate mom a hug. "What is my type, Mom?"

"Beautiful, like Dorothy."

"Yes, Dorothy is gorgeous. John's a lucky guy. I like her very much and they make a great pair. I feel lucky to have them . . . and you . . . all three of you, as my friends."

"Thank you, Justin. You know we feel the same way about you."

Justin held Mom's hand as Dorothy, John and Susan walked toward them. They stood around in a small circle chatting when Justin interrupted the chatter.

"Mom, before I forget, I want to show you something. Let's sit." Justin took the folded catalogue page from his jacket pocket.

"Does this necklace look familiar to you?"

Ruth took the page from Justin. She studied it for a moment before answering. "I was a child at the time but I'll always remember the picture of this unusual necklace. This looks like the one I saw in that picture, so very long ago."

"In Russia?" Justin asked.

"Yes. It was said to belong to the Czar at the time. During the Russian revolution in 1917, rumor was that his daughter, Anastasia and her maid were the only survivors when the entire royal family was executed. Supposedly, they smuggled the jewelry out in the hem of their skirts. There was a big ta-doo about it. Everyone was looking for Anastasia and the jewels. What was the name of that necklace?" Ruth studied the picture some more.

"Was it the Romanov Star?" Susan asked.

Ruth's face lit up. "That's it. It was called the Romanov Star."

"Mom, do you have any idea of the value of that necklace?" Justin asked.

"Oh, my. I suppose it would be worth many millions. It's hard to say. It's very old, from the 18th century and was made for Peter the Great. The Kremlin kept the jewels from that time period locked in a vault, but the Romanov's liked to actually wear them, thus the name. The real name was the Star of the Order of St. Andrew."

Justin looked at Susan. She looked a little pale. "Susan, are you all right? I think you were the owner of a very expensive piece of jewelry. I also think your husband knew what you had and he took off with it."

"Oh my God, Justin. I don't think so. Where would my family ever come in possession of such a piece? We aren't royalty."

"Are any of your relatives Russian?"

"I believe so. Very distantly. I think I recall my mother mentioning that one of my grand-mothers sisters married a Russian military officer. I don't know how I could prove that though. It is a vague memory."

"If that necklace really is the Romanov Star from the time of Peter the Great, it is priceless. Who knows how many people would be after it if they knew it existed. The key to opening this thing up is the Gauvins. I have to get to Richard Gauvin and pin him down. He's a very nervous character. He knows something he's not telling us."

Justin put the picture back in his pocket, done with the conversation for now. "Toody, when do we eat?"

"Right now, Slick." John stood and announced food was being served. At least for the time being, the Romanov Star and the Gauvins were forgotten.

Driving back to the Ritz, Susan flipped the center arm rest up so she could sit closer to Justin. She laid her head on his shoulder. It was nice to have an older car without bucket seats.

"I like your friends, she said. "They're very down-to earth. I like that. I'd like to see them again. Can we?"

"Are you finally realizing that even though I don't move in your circles that I'm still alright, and so are my friends?" He liked the feel of her head on his shoulder. He breathed in the scent of her hair, coconuts and something else he couldn't put his finger on

"I'm so tired." She stifled a yawn. "It's been a long day. I feel like having a glass of wine and going to straight to bed."

His heart raced in his chest. "Is that an invite?"

"No, Justin. It's not. Not yet."

Justin pulled the Caddy to the front door. A doorman opened her side for her and another came around to open his door. He hesitated. "May I walk you to your room?"

"Thanks, but no, Justin. Another time." She kissed him on the cheek, walked through the main doors of the hotel and disappeared.

He sat there looking at the open door of the hotel but not seeing anything. The doorman seemed confused. Was he coming in or not? He pulled away.

First thing in the morning he would pay a visit to Richard Gauvin. It might be a great opportunity to get to him, while Mrs. Gauvin was still in Orlando for three days on a travel agents convention.

Chapter Four

Justin drank his morning coffee and mulled over his edition of the Boston Globe. Even after moving to Florida, he like to read the Globe each morning. Those Florida papers were all feel-good stuff and propaganda in his opinion. One small article caught his attention.

Date line Boston:
An unidentified male was found floating face down in a pond in Boston Common early Thursday morning, said Boston Police Sergeant Doherty. The body was found around 8:00 a.m. Sources indicate the body may have been there for several days. An autopsy will be conducted, but officials have not released any signs indicating the nature of the death.
Could this be the missing Sterling Berns? Maybe he never came to Florida after all. Time for some answers from the nervous Richard Gauvin.

Justin parked his car half way up the block from the Gauvins' house, settled in and waited for some movement. He hated this part of his job. Staking people out for hours on end was a boring job. The Gauvins had awful taste. The mint green siding and brown shutters looked like a blob of mint chocolate chip ice cream. The garage door opened and a car backed out into the street. That was fast. His coffee wasn't even cold yet. As it passed Justin recognized Richard Gauvin. He followed behind by a half block, making sure he wasn't seen. This could be easier than Justin originally thought. It appeared Gauvin was headed for the travel agency. Justin checked his watch. It was two hours before the agency was due to open. Gauvin fumbled with his keys in the front door. Good, it gave Justin time to park and dash toward the door before Gauvin turned and locked it behind him. Justin slipped in sideways as the door closed behind him. When Gauvin turned to lock the door, Justin was already standing inside.

"Shit, you scared the hell of me. We're not open."

Justin crossed his arms across his chest. "I'm quite aware of that. Starting work a little early today? I think we have some unfinished business, off the clock, if you know what I mean?"

Gauvin glanced around. Was he looking for someplace to run or something to use as a weapon? "I'm just getting some paperwork out of the way before the place opens. My wife is in Orlando at a travel agent convention. What the hell are you doing here? I told you before, I don't know anything about Mr. Berns."

"Funny, how I don't believe you." Justin moved within inches of his nose, definitely violating Gauvin's personal space. He watched beads of sweat break out on the weasel's forehead.

Gauvin tried to back away, but cornered himself between his desk and the file cabinet. "Get out, I'm gonna call the police," he said.

"Great, you do that. Maybe you can explain to them the disappearance of Sterling Berns and some very expensive jewels, and one necklace in particular." Justin was close enough to see the small red arteries running through the white of his eyes.

Gauvin breathed out heavily. Damn, he had bad breath. Justin took a step back.

"What necklace?" Gauvin said. Beads of sweat now trickled down his face, weaving through the crevices in his face and dropping in wide circles on his white shirt.

This was just too easy. Justin couldn't resist messing with him just a little. He knew Gauvin would talk with very little muscle. Very casually, Justin took two steps and grabbed him by the throat, almost lifting him off the floor. He could have snapped his little neck without breaking a sweat. *Reign it in, Wade. You're here for information, not to become a felon.* But it would have felt so good. Weasels like that made him sick. "I'm tempted to break your friggin' neck just for the hell of it, but you're not worth it." Justin dropped him to the floor.

He removed the picture of the missing Russian necklace and waved it in front of Gauvin's face. "Go ahead— tell me you don't recognize this. Give me a reason to break your neck. I know you and your wife are involved in the jewel theft and the disappearance of Berns. And since I have a missing person, maybe even his death. Are you a jewel thief and a murderer, Mr. Gauvin?"

Gauvin pulled himself to his feet, grabbing onto the desk top, spilling papers all over the floor. He cleared his throat and rubbed his neck. "Look, I didn't do anything. I don't know what you're talking about."

"Mr. Gauvin, Sergeant Muldoon of the Naples police is a personal friend of mine. He could be here in less than five minutes. So, the way I see this, you have two choices, talk to the police, or talk to me. Which is it going to be?" If only he would give Justin a reason to punch his light outs. It would make his morning.

Gauvin seemed to be considering his options. His eyes darted to the phone on his desk. Did he really think there was time to call someone? Amateurs like that should never get involved in foul play. They didn't have the stomach for it.

"Time's up, Gauvin. You'd better start talking and do what you have to do to clear yourself, if that's possible. Whoever else is involved is far more experienced at this than you. They'll take you down with them. How does spending the next thirty years behind bars for being an accomplice to a murder set with you? Like being a boy toy? My guess is you wouldn't live a month behind bars." Yea, maybe he was laying it on a little thick. It was fun to watch the weasel squirm. "So, I suggest you say something to clear your name or start greasing your asshole."

Gauvin's face turned pale enough to match his shirt. Was he going to puke or pass out? "How . . . how do you know that he's dead?"

Justin smiled. "Ah, progress. So you do know Sterling Berns. Nice to see your memory coming back to you." Justin tossed him the short article from the Boston Globe at him. "Could this be the missing Mr. Berns?"

Gauvin read the article and dropped into his chair. "This isn't proof it was Berns, or that there was any foul play. You can't pin anything on me."

Justin was getting tired of the dance. He sighed. "Let's just say for argument that it is Sterling Berns doing the goldfish shuffle in that pond. You have about two seconds to tell me something that I don't already know or your next trip will be to the Naples police station."

"Look, Mr. Wade. I had nothing to do with his death, if he's really dead. We were simply supplying the buyer for the necklace. Berns was supposed to turn it over to a contact, who in turn, would turn it over to us. Then we provide it to the buyer."

"When did you talk to this contact?"

Gauvin shook his head. "We never heard from him. I guess he made off with the goods. I can tell you, my buyer is pissed. The exchange was supposed to have happened days ago. I have no idea where it is. And nobody said anything about anyone dying."

"What's the necklace worth?"

"We were going to get three million."

"I asked you, what is the thing worth? What was your buyer's price? "

"Fifteen million," said Gauvin.

Justin whistled. Maybe he was in the wrong business. Crime really did appear to pay. "And what were you going to do with it?"

"It was a three-way split. Berns was getting nine million, the contact, two, and we were to get four. Our buyer is a prominent Naples resident. We haven't done anything, because we never heard from the contact."

"Except conspiracy to commit murder and laundering stolen goods. But you could save yourself if you're smart. Tell me the name of your contact."

Gauvin shook his head. "I can't do that, he'll kill us."

"No, he won't, not if I get to him first." Justin reached toward Gauvin's throat again. "Now, I'm done with these games. What's his name?"

"Bucci, His name is Ken B-u-c-c-i, pronounced Bushy. I have no idea where or how to reach him. He usually calls us and keeps us informed of what's going on. We haven't heard from him in days. If he skipped with the goods, we'll never see him again, unless he comes after us."

Ken Bucci? Justin knew that name from a long time ago, back in Revere. *Could it be the same guy?* He was a scum bag then, and probably still was now.

"You can probably get off pretty easy, if I help you. And by all means, be assured that I can help you — if you help me find Bucci. If you hold anything back, I'm going to throw you to the wolves as an accessory to murder."

Justin left him with a punch to the arm. Damn, he was easy to rattle. Let's see how he explained all this to his wife when she gets back from her conference. Justin would like to be a fly on that wall. She was certainly the brains to their operation. Gauvin couldn't keep a secret in a cloister of Buddhist Monks.

What next? Talk to Toody Muldoon and locate this Ken Bucci.

Chapter Five

Light snow fell as Boris Yaakov and Oleg Varyshnikov wiped their feet on the mat before walking through the front door of the Savoy Hotel, the most exclusive hotel in Moscow. Their heels tapped on the gleaming white marble floors. A huge bouquet of fresh flowers on an intricate marble table filled the lobby with a sweet fragrance that aggravated Oleg's allergies. He pulled a linen handkerchief from his breast pocket and stifled a sneeze. Out of old habit, Boris surveyed his surroundings, who was milling about, who was taking notice of their entrance. Why were they meeting at the hotel instead of the Kremlin? It must be something very important, and secretive. They passed the twin alabaster statues that appeared to be holding up the twenty foot ceilings and climbed the stairs to the second floor lounge. The uniformed officer was waiting for them against the far wall in the half darkness of the room. As they approached, he waved in the direction of their seats.

"Good evening Comrade Kaczynski, it is good to see you again," Boris said.

"Yes, yes," the officer responded. He snapped his fingers and two cognacs appeared in front of the men.

"It's been quite some time since we've worked together. We could hash many old memories and talents that we shared. You two are the best. But first, old friends, we need to discuss an operation from which I need your service. That is why I have sent for you."

"I assumed as much," Boris said. Why else would he have called them out of retirement? "But I think I can speak for both of us when I say we'd be most happy to help in any way we can." He took a sip of his cognac and nodded his approval. "We've been quite bored since the new regime has taken over and disbanded our operations."

"Yes, Comrade Kaczynski," Oleg added, tapping his glass in salute to the officer.

"Good, let's get down to business," Comrade Kaczynski said. He pulled his chair closer to the gleaming mahogany table. "Word has reached me that a necklace that belonged to Anastasia Romanov, the daughter of Czar Nicholas the Second has turned up in America. It's been missing since the revolution of 1917, when the Imperial family were toppled. It's worth millions in American dollars and I want it. If you can retrieve it, we will split at least fifteen million American dollars between us."

"Ah," Oleg said with a smile. "I was hoping for a vacation. I've missed the good restaurants we enjoyed in America. It has been a long time since we ate as well as we did during our last stay there."

"I'm sure with five mil a piece, you can return to America and eat very well for a very long time."

Boris and Oleg looked at each other for a moment. "Da," they answered in unison.

"Wasn't Anastasia the daughter they never found any remains from when the family bodies were exhumed in 1991?" Boris asked.

"So," said Kaczynski, "I see that you know our history. That is true. There's been much speculation as to the whereabouts of the mysterious Anastasia. It's possible that she and her maid escaped along with many of the jewels and that her descendants are now living in America. But that is of no concern to me. The necklace in question is called the Romanov Star and is worth millions. The legacy is of no concern to me, I only want the money."

"When do we start?" Boris said with a smile.

"Wonderful," Comrade Kaczynski beamed. "I'll give you all the information I have. I have it locked away. Meet me here tomorrow morning at ten o'clock and I will fill you in and we can discuss how this should be handled."

"I don't know this story." Oleg said to Boris after the meeting with Comrade Kacynski. "Could this necklace really be from the 18th century?"

"That is the mystery. The Romanov's were in power just prior to the revolution. It is said that the Romanov's physician awakened the family and told them they were in grave danger. The family dressed and followed him to what they thought was a safe location. They were ordered into a small cell and at that time, they knew the physician had betrayed them. An execution squad arrived and opened fire.

The women crossed their arms across their chest to protect themselves, but they all fell. The last said to die was Anastasia and her maid."

Boris paused, letting the story settle in Oleg's mind.

"This is where it gets interesting," Boris continued. "According to legend, the family was also speared with bayonets, however, Anastasia and the Grand Duchess Olga were protected by the diamonds and jewels sewn into their clothing. When the guards were later sent to dispose of the bodies, Anastasia, the maid and many of the jewels were missing. The Romanov Star has 24 carats of diamonds in it. If it is the real deal, we could be very rich men very soon, my dear friend."

Chapter Six

Justin rang the bell on the chocolate colored door to the Gauvin's house. No answer. He pounded a few times. Nothing. The gate leading to the back yard was ajar. Justin pushed it open and spotted Richard Gauvin, sprawled nude on a chaise lounge by his pool. "Mr. Gauvin. Sorry for bothering you again, but there's a few questions I would like to clear up."

He cleared his throat, giving the man a chance to cover his nakedness. There was no movement. Justin cautiously approached the man. Still no movement.

"Mr. Gauvin," he said a little louder. Still no response. Justin noticed blood on the cement deck. It appeared to be coming from the back of the man's neck. He checked Gauvin's wrist and felt for a pulse. Again nothing. Damn, he wasn't sleeping. He was dead. So much for more questions. Wrapping his finger with a clean handkerchief, he rolled Gauvin's head to the side. A puncture wound, round and symmetrical. About the size of an icepick.

"I guess I wasn't the only one that wanted to get to him," he said aloud to no one. Why wasn't the body sun-burned? He pushed his finger on the skin, judging the amount of rigor mortis. Best guess was less than an hour. He reached for the phone located on the table in front of the dead man and quickly stopped himself. Don't be so stupid, Wade. Fingerprints.

He looked around. Would the killer still be in the house? He reached for his weapon, which he wasn't wearing. "Shit" he murmured. "Not a good time to be unarmed". He swept the property by eye, first around the lush grounds and then inside the house. Thank God it was empty. He pulled out his cell and called Toody Muldoon at his home.

Three Naples police cars, sirens blaring and blue lights flashing, came to an abrupt stop in front of the Gauvin home. Muldoon and five uniformed officers met Justin at the front door. The largest one brushed passed Justin, his shoulder brushing against his, with not even a nod.

"Well, excuse me" Justin said with a snide look at the large man as the man continued on into the house.

"Stick around, Justin," Toody said. "I'm sure the watch commander will want to speak with you. I told him what was going on, so don't sweat it."

"Okay, John." Justin was careful not to call his friend Toody when he was on duty. "Who's the big guy? He brushed me aside without acknowledging me. I'm not going anywhere. This case is getting hairier by the minute. I've got a missing husband, stolen jewels, and now a dead suspect. It may be time to start carrying again. I sure hate carrying a gun in this weather."

"That's the commander," John said. "I sometimes wish I were back in uniform on these humid days. When I'm plain clothes I have to wear this damn jacket and I all but melt. Let's take a look at the body."

"I'll be inside here, where it's cool. If your commander wants me I'll be in the living room." He'd already seen the body, and it was getting riper by the second in that ninety degree late afternoon sun.

Justin watched John do his own sweep of the interior. Upon not finding anything of significance, he exited through the triple wide opening of the pocketed glass doors onto the lanai, looking up, down, and around as he went. A uniformed officer with camera in hand, snapped photos of every room.

John returned with the Incredible Hulk that brushed by Justin earlier. "Justin, this is Lieutenant Chambers. I've filled him in with everything I know. If there's anything else you can add that may have transpired since you talked to me last, why don't you fill him in?"

"I have nothing to add, Lieutenant Chambers," Justin said. "Nothing's happened since I talked to John. I decided to drop in on Mr. Gauvin, to see what else I could squeeze out of him. There was no answer at the door so I walked around back through the open gate and found him just as you saw him. I called John right away. Do you have cause of death?"

"Head wound of some kind. But I'm sure you'll get that information from John when it becomes available. I realize you're working on a case, but I'd appreciate it if you stay out of the way of my people. Do you understand what I'm saying?"

"Perfectly," Justin answered. "Am I free to go now?"

"Of course," Lieutenant Chambers replied.

"And by the way," Justin said, "There are some ladies things in the bedroom. Not exactly the kind you'd expect to find on Mrs. Gauvin, if you know what I mean." He raised his eyebrows and winked at Toody.

Visions of Mrs. Gauvin in the flimsy cover-ups made Justin suppress a gag. "Any idea where Mrs. Gauvin is?"

"Not a clue," the lieutenant replied, "but if you find out, let me know."

At least Justin knew one thing that the police did not. The Gauvin's secretary was easy to pull information from. He already knew that Rochelle Gauvin was supposed to be in Orlando at a three day travel agency conference. This would give him a short advantage over the cops before they gleaned the same information from the gum-chomping receptionist.

Chapter Seven

Flight 1769 from London arrived at Boston's Logan Airport twenty minutes late. Boris and Oleg disembarked and followed the parade of people leaving the plane to the baggage pickup area. Neither spoke during the boring twenty minute wait for their bags to come through. After picking up their bags they entered a hotel shuttle and headed for the Hilton Hotel on the grounds of the airport, where they made their first phone call in their attempt to find their contact. Boris allowed the phone to ring ten times before he hung up.

Twenty minutes later Boris called again. The call connected immediately.

"Helga? This is Boris. Yes, we just got in. Tell me what you know," Boris requested.

"Good evening, Boris. Can't you at least wish me a good evening? I am doing this job for you for no money. You can at least be pleasant . . . Yes?"

"I'm sorry, Helga. I suppose I'm being a bit overanxious. I hope you are well. Give my regards to your husband. He is a good man. I like him, and was sorry to see him defect to America. But, now I wish him well."

"Thank you, Boris. He spoke well of you, also. He did enjoy working for you, but he felt it was time. I'm sure you understand." For a moment, there was silence on her end of the line. "He filed for divorce shortly after we arrived here."

"Oh, I'm sorry to hear that Helga. To tell you the truth, you were too good for him. But now, Helga. I need that information."

"Yes, of course. The man's name was Sterling Berns, but he's dead. The police found him last week in the park. There was a middle man. His name is Ken Bucci. I haven't been able to locate his address. He spends a great amount of time at the Suffolk Downs horse racing track in the part of Boston called East Boston. Any taxi driver can take you there. He also spends time at Nat's Pool Room, in Revere. If you check your front desk for mail you will find an envelope there with his picture. It's a few years old but I was told he still looks the same. Now tell me, Boris. I don't want to know what sort of case you are working on but I'd like to know if it is official business or not, just for my own protection."

"I can't tell you anything, Helga. Just believe me, it's very important. Don't worry. Nobody will be looking over your pretty shoulder. You see, I do remember how beautiful you are."

"Oh! I didn't think you ever noticed anything about me."

He could hear the smile in her voice.

"Maybe you and I missed something, Boris. Do you think so?"

Boris felt his cheeks warm and a smile crossed his face too. "Probably, Helga. I thought of it when we were working together but I was always too involved in my work. I never would have let that bastard Ivan get you.

He is an idiot to have divorced you."

"Maybe before you leave America, Boris, we could see each for pleasure, not business."

"That would be wonderful, Helga. I promise to be in touch before we leave."

"Goodbye, Boris."

Boris turned and saw Oleg sitting on the edge of the bed, amused by the one sided conversation he'd been listening to. He shrugged. "I've always had a thing for her. But I let her marry that asshole Ivan when I was trying to climb the KGB ladder. I was always too busy for her."

"Now is the time, Boris. If I were in your shoes, I'd be going over to see her right now."

"We have a job to do, Oleg. Let's get this done first. It's going to be difficult to find this Bucci guy with only a photograph to go by,"

"We'll find him, Boris. We always do."

"Yes," Boris whispered, as he gazed out the hotel window, thinking more about the woman he let get away than the job at hand. "We always do."

Early next morning their black Chevrolet Caprice was parked off to the side, facing the turn stiles at Suffolk Downs Racetrack. Stupid gamblers. Why would people throw their hard earned money away, like that, on a horse race? At least with women or drugs, you had a chance to having something left at the end of the day.

Oleg looked at his Chinese made, ten dollar watch. They'd been sitting in their rented car for three hours and twenty minutes. He needed to take a piss and they weren't seeing anyone that looked like Bucci.

"There," said Boris. "I think that's him. Look, Oleg. Do you agree?"

Oleg took the binoculars from Boris and adjusted them to his poor eyesight. "Yes, that's him. I can tell by his curly hair and stooped shoulders."

"Come, Oleg. We must follow him so he doesn't get away."

They followed Bucci into the racetrack and sat three rows behind him. When Bucci went to the betting window, one of them followed him. Every time Bucci went to place a bet, they watched him from two different directions making sure that he couldn't give them the slip. He never won.

Two hours later, Bucci left the park. They trailed him and as he parked in front of an apartment building on the corner of Nahant and Shirley Avenues, in a town called Revere.

Bucci entered the building through the front door. They quickly followed, careful not to lose him in one of the apartments.

They were spotted in the doorway of the building. Boris turned toward the closest apartment door and fiddled with his keys while speaking to Oleg in Russian. Hopefully, the man would think they were new tenants in the building.

Bucci continued to his apartment down the hall. When he turned the lock on the door and opened it, Boris and Oleg lunged for the door before it closed. They both shouldered against the door, Bucci sprawled into the apartment, falling against the arm of his sofa and bounced onto the floor. As Boris shut the door, Oleg pounced on the man on the floor and twisted his arm behind his back. He dragged the little man to his feet. Boris faced Bucci and said, "Gospodin (*Mr.*) Bucci, I am not a patient man, and I will stand for no nonsense and will spend no time pleading for your cooperation. We want the Romanov

Star. Now!"

"I . . . I don't know what ya talking about," Bucci stammered.

Boris grabbed him by the throat and squeezed. "I want the necklace. If you don't give it to me, now . . ." He shook his head. "Oleg, tie him up. I'm not going to waste any time with him."

Oleg pulled some plastic tie-wraps from his pocket. He quickly tied Bucci's hands behind his back and pushed him down onto the sofa and tie-wrapped his feet.

Boris took a pair of surgical pliers from his jacket pocket, grabbed Bucci by the shoulder and turned him face down on the sofa.

Oleg leaned over and whispered in the man's ear, "He warned you. You should do what he asks. This is going to be very painful."

"One more time, Gospodin Bucci," Boris said. "Give me the necklace."

"I don't know . . . I don't know," Bucci sobbed. "What ya talking about? I don't have no necklace."

Oleg pushed Bucci's face into the sofa to muffle the scream.

Boris grabbed one bound hand. He gripped a fingernail with the pliers and pulled as hard as he could until the nail left the finger, spurting blood over the sofa.

Soon he'd be telling them what they wanted to know.

Boris wrapped a towel around the bleeding finger and flipped Bucci over to face him.

"Now, Gospodin Bucci. Do I have to do that again or will you cooperate?"

The man writhed in pain.

"I'll repeat the question, once. If I don't receive a

reply I'll ask you a second time. I will not ask a third. Did I make myself clear?"

Bucci nodded.

Imbecile. Why couldn't he just cooperate? "Did I make myself clear, Gospodin Bucci?"

"Yea," he answered. "I'll talk. It's in Florida. I sent it there a couple a days ago. My partner has it. She's probably passed to the buyer already."

"She? Who is she supposed to pass it to?" Oleg asked.

"I don't know . . . some rich guy."

"How did you get your hands on it," Boris asked.

"I was just da middle man. It was given ta me to pass along."

Boris sighed. He was losing his patience. "From whom? Who did you get it from?"

"His name was Berns."

Berns. That matched what Helga said.

"How did he die?"

"He was strangled."

Oleg shoved the man and he fell sideways on the sofa. "How do you know this?"

"I did it," Bucci said into the seat cushion.

Boris straightened him into a sitting position. "I see. Wasn't he your partner?"

"Yea."

"So, you double-crossed him. Why?"

"He wanted to cut me out."

"You Americans have a name for a person like yourself. It's called a piece of shit. Look at you. You're missing a fingernail . . . which you didn't have to lose. All you had to do is tell me what I wanted to know. Should I kill you too, or will you keep your mouth shut about our little visit."

"I, I can't go to the police. I killed a man. Don't kill me." He pleaded. "Just untie me. I promise . . . there's nothing I can do now. Let me go, please!"

"It's your lucky day. I'm going to let you live . . . if you give me the name of your partner in Florida."

"Okay, okay," he sighed. A little color flushed back in his cheeks.

"Her name is Rochelle Gauvin. She owns a travel agency in Naples. Florida. The name of the agency is Bruce Travel. I have her phone number in my desk somewhere."

"That's good. She'd better still have the necklace . . . if you want to live," Oleg said.

"Untie him, Oleg." Boris faced the man. "Remember what I told you, any police and you are dead."

"I won't, I won't," Bucci moaned.

Boris and Oleg left. Oleg gave Boris directions back to the Hilton Hotel from the maps supplied by the car rental agency. They called the concierge and requested flight reservations to Naples, Florida.

Thirty minutes later the phone rang. A Jet Blue flight was leaving in two hours and although the plane was full, he was able to get them two seats. They'd be making a connection in Orlando, with a one hour layover, enabling them to fly right into the small Naples airport as opposed to going to the larger Fort Myers International airport. The tickets would be waiting for them at check in.

They checked out, leaving a hefty envelope for the concierge.

Chapter Eight

Justin knocked on Susan's hotel room door. He peeked through the peep hole from the hallway and saw a blurred eye looking back at him from the inside. The door opened, as the startling beauty of Susan Berns, in a lounging robe, filled the doorway. Holy Crap. She was a knock-out.

She didn't speak but stood aside indicating he should come in. A provocative smile crossed her lips. The phone rang and jolted him out of the fantasy already playing out in his mind. Susan picked up the phone and after a short conversation, handed him the receiver. "It's for you."

Justin took the phone, his rough hand covering her soft one for a moment. A spark coursed through his body and settled in his groin, instantly making his trousers too tight. Was she laughing at him behind those mesmerizing eyes or did she feel that same spark?

"Justin. Are you listening?" It was his friend, John.

Justin shook his head to clear his mind. "Yea, what's up?" He listened as John told him that the coroner had examined Richard Gauvin's body. "You're not going to like this. Gauvin wasn't ice-picked in the back of his head. He was shot with a .22 caliber slug."

"A .22 caliber? That's a hit, John. This case is getting more intriguing by the day.

"I agree," John said. "This is getting out of hand. You realize, of course, that the Naples police are now involved in this all the way. Also, the examiner estimated that the body had been laying in the sun for over six hours.

"God, that'd be ripe. Why wasn't he a Krispy Kreme donut by then?"

"Ahh, see that's why I'm smarter than you," replied John. "When the body dies, so do the inflammatory cells. The body won't burn or blister. They just turn to dust eventually."

"Touché. That's one point for you. But don't let it go to your head."

"I didn't know it either, until someone explained it to me during another case. I'll let you go. Sorry to disrupt your evening with the lovely lady, but I thought the timeline and cause of death might be important to you."

"Yes, they are. Thanks. I'll be in touch." Turning away from Susan, Justin spoke quietly into the receiver, "Have you heard anything further about that killing in Boston?"

"Yes, I have. It was Sterling Berns. He was strangled. The Boston Police are investigating. If I hear any more, I'll let you know. I wasn't sure this was the right time to give you this news, but you asked."

"That's fine, John. We'll talk later." Justin rested the phone in its cradle and walked over to Susan. He placed his hand on her arm. He struggled to keep his face nonchalant. It wasn't every day he was entertaining a beautiful woman when he found out her husband was strangled. Should he tell her? Not yet. Couldn't he have a little time with her first, before he broke the news?

"Susan, I've missed you. You've been on my mind all day. Ever since John's party, I couldn't get you out of my mind."

"I missed you too, Justin," she whispered, as she slid into his arms. They kissed, tenderly at first, then the passion began to rise. They separated and she took his hand and started to lead him toward the bedroom.

"No," Justin said, as he stopped her. Damn his conscience. "Susan I'd give my right arm to spend the next few hours in that bedroom with you. But there's something I have to tell you. I don't want you to think I'm holding anything back. Please sit down." He walked her over to the divan under the window. He took her hand.

"What is it Justin? You're scaring me."

How was she going to take this? He'd told lots of people bad news like this, but not anyone he cared deeply about. "John just informed me that your husband was found dead in Boston. He'd been strangled. I'm sorry."

Her shoulders drooped, she let go of his hand and covered her face with her hands. "Oh, Justin," she cried. "That poor man. At one time I loved him very much. He was my husband for ten years."

She cried softly for a few minutes, then she straightened up and wiped her eyes. "I'll grieve for him but he brought all this upon himself. He was such a foolish man. You said he was in Boston? I was sure he had come here. I need some time to think."

Justin nodded. What else could he expect? "Shall I leave, Susan?"

She shook her head. "No. Stay with me. Right now I think I need you."

"I'll be here for you, Susan."

Justin sat beside her and Susan buried her head against his shoulder, crying on and off for about an hour. She could stay there all night as far as he was concerned. There was the smell of coconuts from her hair and an expensive perfume from her neck. Chanel No. 5. That was it.

Finally, her crying subsided.

"Can I do anything for you?" he asked.

"Yes," she lifted her head so he could see her eyes glistening with tears. "Take me into the bedroom."

Justin swept her into his arms, kissed her long and hard and carried her through the doorway. He found, as he laid her down on the bed, that she was naked under her robe. He reached down and undid the satin sash and splayed the robe open. He gasped as he stared down at the most gorgeous body he had ever seen. She was perfect and he could see that she wanted him to see her this way.

"Susan, you're so beautiful."

"Whatever I am, Justin, I'm all yours now," she purred.

Justin tenderly kissed her breast, her neck and nibbled on her body as he slowly lowered himself until he was kissing her on her thighs. She moaned as she parted her legs and he moved his mouth to that sweet spot. It didn't take long for her to reach a fever pitch and groan in ecstasy as her body arched and shivered.

When she calmed, he stood, quickly undressed and pulled her on top of him. She guided him into her and she lifted herself up so he could take in the vision above him. She rode him hard and long, almost angrily, until they reached their peak together, moaning and shivering as one, with Justin exploding into her.

They stayed bound to each other until he was soft. She rolled off and they lay face to face, looking into each other's eyes.

It was a few moments before Justin spoke. "Somehow I knew it would be like that. There was something in your eye's that told me so." He nibbled on her neck.

She responded quietly. "You drove me almost crazy. You do that quite well. I have only had that done to me just twice before, but not as well as you."

"Twice?" She couldn't be talking about intercourse. *Oh that. Wade, sometimes your stupidity even amazes me.*

"I'd like you to do that again, sometime soon," she said softly into his ear.

"You're my inspiration." He laughed. "I'll do it all again, and again and again. If you'll only give me a few minutes." Justin smiled sheepishly.

"Promise?" Justin and Susan promised each other four more times before they went to sleep for the night, with Susan cuddled in his arms.

Justin woke to the noise of water running in the bathroom. He rolled out of bed dragging a blanket from the bed to wrap around his waist. He stopped at the doorway and watched Susan, her back to the shower door, washing her hair. She turned to see him staring at her through the frosted glass. She opened the door slightly and crooked her finger to invite him in.

"I'd love to . . . but tonight's another night and I have some things to do early this morning. You stopped me from doing my job last night, so I have to handle it now, while I'm still able to. Will tonight be a repeat of last night?"

She pouted, and bit down on her lower lip "Justin, I have to go to Boston. No matter how things were between Sterling and I, I owe it to him to be there. I'll be back as soon as possible. I have a lot to do up there. I promise. . . I'll call you as soon as I know when I'll be back."

The last thing he wanted to do was leave her standing naked in that shower. But if he was honest, his member could use a break. "Okay. Keep me informed. I'll be here waiting. I have things to do too. This case is getting very interesting, now." Too many people were dying and he didn't like it. Hell, he would be next, or Susan. Should he tell her about the execution of Richard Gauvin? He didn't want to scare her. "Do you want John to set up some protection for you up there?"

"I'll handle it, don't worry about me." She closed the door to the shower and continued her morning routine.

Maybe he'd make that call to Boston himself and get her some protection whether she wanted it or not.

Justin drove to the Bruce Travel Agency as two bulky looking men walked to the door of the agency. They looked like the many Germans who had found their paradise called Naples, Florida. He'd wait until the tourists had booked their flight back home. He pulled his car into the lot next to the agency as he saw something hit the large glass door from the inside. Something was wrong. He bounded from his car and dashed to the front door, shouldering his way in.

A man was standing over Rochelle Gauvin, who was cowering on the floor.

"Okay, that's enough!" He reached under his armpit for his snub nosed .38 caliber revolver. God damn.

He'd left it at home when he went to Susan's the night before.

He took one step toward the men when he felt something heavy hit his head and shatter his consciousness. Justin dropped. When he awoke, Rochelle was lying beside him. He checked her pulse. She was alive, but bleeding from the side of her head. Blood ran down her cheek, soaking into the rug. She moaned as Justin turned her over.

"Thank God," he said aloud. He put his hand to his own head. Blood covered his palm when he pulled it away. And it hurt like hell. He staggered to his feet and wet his handkerchief in the lavatory sink. He wiped her face, making her stir, then open her eyes.

"Oh, my God! I thought they were going to kill me."

"Who were they, Mrs. Gauvin? What did they want from you?"

"I— I don't know. They were foreigners. I have no idea why they did this to me."

This was not the time for secrecy. These people meant business. "You're not telling me the truth, Mrs. Gauvin. I'm sorry that your husband is dead. But so is Sterling Berns, and there's a still the matter of the missing necklace. These people don't mind killing people. Are you really going to stick to your story that you don't know anything? "

"I don't know, I don't know," she said wearily. "I never saw them before. Please, call an ambulance. I think . . ."

Justin caught her as she passed out again. He called 911.

Justin stood in the doorway as Lieutenant Chambers and John entered. Justin shrugged his shoulders at John. *I know, I know, I'm always around when men get killed and ladies get beat up.*

John walked back to Justin, "She wasn't shot, slick, she just had a whack to the side of her head. This case is getting out of control now."

"I know, I know," Justin replied.

By the way, where is Susan?"

"She's up north, seeing to her husband's funeral."

"What do you think, Justin? Is she involved in this in any way?"

"Don't be ridiculous. May I remind you that she hired me to look for her husband and the necklace? If she was involved, why would she be asking me for help?"

John nodded. "Remember what Lieutenant Chambers said?"

"No, I haven't forgotten. But I've been in on this case from the start. I'll stay out of their way as much as I can. But, John, between you and me—this is my livelihood and it's involving Susan and maybe even my life. I have to stick with this. You know this. Will you still be able to feed me information?"

"It depends," John said. "Depends on what we find out. In the meantime. I'm asking you to keep us informed. Chambers is a real hard-ass. He'll bust you for the slightest thing . . . so be careful. Feed him something from time to time. Try to stay on the good side of him . . . well, at least on his better side."

Yea, and he knew where he could insert his foot. What an asshole. Justin hated cops that thought their information should be confidential, but his should be public knowledge.

"What does Chambers think of all this?"

"He has no idea at this point, Justin. What we do know is that they had accents. Not Italian or German. She said they sounded Russian."

"Russian, huh? That's interesting," Justin said. "The Romanov Star necklace came from Russia. There has to be a connection. And John, thanks for asking about my head. I was clobbered pretty hard, you know. He hit me with a gun."

John laughed and gave him a good-natured slap on the back. "I didn't ask because I knew that if you were hit on the head, you were all right. Not much can damage that thick skull of yours. Slick."

"Thanks, pal. I'll catch you later. Hey, have you noticed? Those damn tourists are back."

"Now that you live here they're damn tourists, huh? But when you came down to visit me a few years back, you were one of them, a damn snowbird! I'll catch you later."

Justin smiled as he slipped his cell into his pocket. John was a good man. He had a nice family, a beautiful wife and a great mother-in-law. Justin could use a woman like Dorothy at this stage of his life. Maybe Susan could be his Dorothy. That wouldn't be half bad, maybe better than half bad.

The phone was ringing as Justin walked through his office door. It was his real estate friend, Robert McNally At one time he and Mack used to have drinks after work. Justin didn't have any prejudice against gays, but sometimes Mack kind of creeped him out. Mack may have liked him a little too much. They weren't that good of friends.

"Justin darling, I found the perfect office for you. The owner of the building at the corner of Goodlette and

Golden Gate has one office space left and wants it rented ASAP. He's putting the building up for sale and wants to show it to prospective clients with full occupancy."

"What's the space like?" Justin knew the building. It wasn't new, but it had been updated. Anything had to be an improvement of the dump he had now.

"Darling, it's wonderful." Robert drawled. "Meets all your criteria and they'll pay for any build-out. Triple net rent, of course, but that's standard."

Justin had too much on his plate to worry too much about his office space right now. He told his friend he'd take it if the price was right. And please, stop calling him Darling.

Justin relaxed back in his chair, his feet on his desk, and his hands behind his head. If Sterling Berns was dead, Richard Gauvin was dead, the Russians were sniffing around, and Rochelle Gauvin really didn't know where the necklace was, then who did?

"I really should go home and get some shut eye," he mumbled, as he drifted off to sleep in his chair. He awoke two hours later knowing what his next move should be. He had seen it in his dream.

Boston . . . that's where he should be. If Sterling Berns took the necklace to pass off, then somebody up there must have been involved with him. Bucci. He shook the cobwebs from his head. How had he forgotten about Bucci?

Chapter Nine

Justin put a call to Susan's cell, "Hi, Hon. How are you doing?"

"Who is this?" she asked. He could hear the confusion in her voice.

"What do you mean, who is this? It's Justin." Who the hell did she think it was?

"Oh, I'm sorry. I didn't recognize your voice. I'm sorry, Justin. Where are you?"

"I'm here, at Logan Airport."

She barked back at him. "What the hell are you doing here? Checking up on me?"

Whoa! Back up lady. She was supposed to be pleased he was there. What was with the attitude? "Why would I be checking up on you?"

"I'm working on a case. YOUR case. Did you forget that?"

"I'm sorry. You just took me by surprise. Have you found out anything?"

She sounded distracted. What was going on? "I've got a lead— up here. Have you found anything?" If she wanted to be all business, he could do that. At least his head could. Not so sure about the rest of his body.

"Only this," she said, "I found something on Sterling's note pad. There are a few names I don't recognize. I knew most of his business associates and friends. He always talked about the things he did and the people he met. But there's a name here I don't know. Bucci? It could be something, or it could be nothing."

"Susan, I'm still at baggage claim, but I'll grab my bags and be right over. Okay?"

"Yes, you have my address. I'm sorry I was short, Justin, I missed you terribly."

"I'm on the way." Women. He'd never understand them.

When the taxi pulled into her drive, he let out a whistle. Its grandeur easily matched the mansions on Gulfshore Drive in Naples. She greeted him in a long embrace.

Susan leaned into him and whispered, "I've become even more wealthy, Justin. It seems Sterling had more life insurance than I knew about. I suppose you want to marry me now, huh?"

"Not on your life." Justin laughed. "I prefer them poor and homeless."

She pulled him into the house and shut the door.

They sat in the parlor discussing the case. It was hard for Justin to sit next to her without grabbing her. Her flimsy robe kept gaping open and he couldn't keep his eyes off her exposed breasts. Justin stood. "I have to check on something. Would you drive me or should I rent a car?"

She pulled the robe closed in front of her. "I'll take you. Where am I taking you?"

"Revere," he answered. "I have to find that man called Bucci. I may know him. If it's the same person, it'll be quite a meeting. It looks like he was the middle man in an exchange of the necklace between your husband and a buyer in Naples."

"Sterling wouldn't have tried to sell my necklace. Is that what you are saying?"

"That's how it appears, Susan. Bucci and I grew up together in Revere. We hung out in the same crowd, but we never got along. If he's the same guy, he's probably hanging around the same pool room that was there when I was a kid."

Susan excused herself to change and they climbed in to her little BMW Z4 convertible.

They headed for the Ted Williams Tunnel which took them through East Boston and into Revere.

He gave her directions to Nat's pool room. She parked across the street from the entrance and was about to leave the car to follow him in.

"Oh no!" Justin said. "You're waiting here, Sweetie. You don't want to go into that place. When I was a kid I remember a girl that went in there. They called her Dirty Gerty, and she did the entire pool room. Are you interested in that?"

Susan quickly sat back in the car.

Justin looked around for the owner. Nate was sitting at the far end of the bar, a beer in his hand even though it was still mid-morning. His once thick black hair was now silver and he put on forty or fifty pounds since Justin last saw him. Justin sat beside him on a stool and ordered coffee. He turned to Nate and asked if he had seen Ken Bucci recently lately? Nate replied that he hadn't seen him recently but word on the street was that Bucci had been mugged and was recuperating at home. He told Justin where Bucci was living now, but not knowing which apartment he had.

Justin gave Susan directions down Shirley Avenue to the large brick apartment.

She looked around at the neighborhood. Not exactly any place she'd like to call home. "You grew up here?" she asked.

"Just stay in the car. Put the top up and lock the doors." She really was a stuck up bitch sometimes. He found Bucci's name on the mail slot and rang the bell three times.

"Who the hell is it?" a voice came through the intercom.

"Ken Bucci?" Justin asked.

"That's me. Who da hell are you?"

"Justin Wade."

"Don't know no Wade. Go away."

"Yes, you do. Think back a few years. We played ball together. I punched your face in a few time."

"Goddamn. Yeah. I 'member now. But I think I was da one doing da face smashing."

The door buzzed which allowed entrance into the building. Justin walked up to the second floor. Ken Bucci was standing just inside the doorway of his apartment.

"You're just as ugly as ever," Justin said as he held his hand.

Bucci looked down at his bandaged finger and shook his head.

"What happened to you?" Justin asked.

"None of your friggin' business. What cha doin' here? I heard you left town years ago."

"I think you're involved in something that may be over your head. Is that the work of the some Russian guests?" Justin pointed toward Bucci's hand.

"Russians? What? Are you, crazy? This had nuttin' ta do with no Russians. What business is it of yours, anyway?"

"Ken, I'm a private detective now. I'm working on a case. I was hired to find Sterling Berns and a certain heirloom, antique Russian necklace. And you, my friend are involved."

Bucci pushed Justin with his good arm. "Get da fuck outta here! I don't know nuttin' bout a fucking necklace!"

"Ken," Justin said quietly. "You're going to tell me where that necklace is. I'm not leaving here until you do." He slipped his watch off and placed it in his pocket.

"I told ya, Wade. I ain't never seen no Russians. But I've got my own goons. One call and you'll be floatin' in the ocean."

"Is that so?" Justin grabbed Bucci by the throat, "I never liked you as a kid, and I don't like you now. I want two questions answered. Who killed Sterling Berns and where is the necklace?"

"Fuck you. I ain't telling you nuttin'."

Justin's right hand smashed into Bucci's nose. Blood spurted over Justin's shirt and continued to run from Bucci's nose, as he slumped to the floor. Justin turned Bucci over shoving his face into the dirty wooden floor. He put one knee into the small of Bucci's back and held his bandaged hand out. "Ken, we don't have to do this. Tell me what I want to know. I'm not a cop and I don't have any intention of turning you in to the police. This is between you and me. Tell me where the necklace is."

Bucci was spitting blood. "I don't know what ya talking 'bout."

Justin pulled Bucci's hand closer to his body, close enough to lean his other knee on his bandaged hand.

Bucci screamed in pain. "Okay, okay. You win."

As Justin loosened his grip and started to rise, Bucci quickly rolled over spitting blood and swinging his arms. He caught Justin on the side of his head, almost knocking him over.

Justin quickly recovered and shot his fist into Bucci's midsection, doubling him over. Justin's fist found the side of Bucci's face making him fall like a sack of potatoes. He grabbed Bucci by the throat, pulling him to his feet and into the tiny kitchen. Dirty pots, glasses and food lay everywhere. Justin rummaged through the drawers until he found what looked like the sharpest knife.

He shoved Bucci up against the wall. "Kenny old friend. If you don't tell me what I want to know, right now, I'm going to cut your balls off."

Bucci's eyes got wide, but only blood poured from his nose, nothing from his mouth, not the words Justin needed to hear.

Justin stuck the point of the knife through his pants and slashed sideways, creating a large hole at his crotch. He put the knife back against the bulge in Bucci's tighty whities.

"Ever have any kids? 'Cause your about to lose your manhood. Say goodbye to your balls."

"Okay . . . okay! I'll talk." he said through a mouthful of blood. "But you're too late. The Russians beat you to it. They're the ones that pulled my fingernail off."

Damn. He was afraid of that. "Who killed Sterling Berns?" Justin asked

"I did. I strangled the bastard. He was gonna cut me out and make the trade himself. He wanted all the money."

Justin let up on the knife against his crotch, but held him pinned against the wall. "How did you know this Sterling Berns?"

"I didn't know him. I was given a picture of him."

"You killed a man from a picture? Did you get the necklace?"

"Yeah. It was him. He looked like him and he was carrying identification. I checked, after he was dead." Bucci chuckled.

This is funny? "Where is the necklace, Ken?"

"I sent it to a lady in Florida, a Rochelle Gauvin."

"When did you send it . . . and how?"

"I sent it last week by UPS. Certified. She signed for it."

A multi-million dollar necklace and he sends it by UPS. What a moron. "Okay, you shit head," Justin sneered. "Talk to me about the Russians that did that little job on you."

He held up his bandaged finger. "Two Russians, they came and asked the same questions. They did this ta me 'cause I didn't wanna talk. Yanked my Goddamn fingernail right off wit a pair of pliers."

"But you did, right? You told them the necklace was in Florida?"

"Yeah, you bastard. They probably already have it."

Justin pushed him into a dirty kitchen chair. Bucci slumped over the table.

Justin called the Naples Police Department from his cell. He waited until John Muldoon came to the phone.

"John, this is Justin. Look, I'm here near Boston. I'll grab the first plane back to Florida, but you have to act fast on this for me. Those two Russians aren't going to stop until that have that necklace. Put Mrs. Gauvin in protective custody or do whatever you have to do to keep her alive. Save her, John, if it's not too late. I'll come as soon as I can."

"I'll do what I can, Justin. Can you tell me more?"

"No time, John. You better hurry. She got off easy last time because I interrupted them. The Russians are already in Naples."

"Okay, Justin. Chambers is going to want some answers. Take care."

Justin turned to Bucci. "You were always a shit-head, Ken. You were a wise-mouth back then, and nothing's changed. The last thing I heard, you were into drugs. You've not changed a bit, loser then, loser now."

Susan look startled as he entered the car, blood spattered all over him. "My God, what happened, Justin?"

He looked down at his blood stained shirt. "Not my blood. His, just a little persuading. He was the Ken Bucci I knew as a kid."

Should he tell her now that this douche bag killed her husband? She deserved the truth. "That guy killed your husband, Susan. He confessed to me."

Susan jammed the brakes on and skidded to a stop. "Aren't we going to call the police?"

"Not right now. I'll give the information to John and let them go through the right authorities. Bucci won't get away with it. We can't turn him in because we'd be involved. I don't want anybody to know we were here. He won't say anything. He can't. He's got a rap sheet already."

"Are you okay, Justin?"

"Hell, I'm fine."

"You're bleeding from your eye. Did he hit you?"

"Yeah, he sucker punched me when I started to let him up. I'm fine. Are you really concerned about me?"

"Of course, Justin." She leaned over and kissed him.

Justin squeezed her knee. "That's nice. I like to hear things like that from you, Susan. I've got to get back to Naples right away. You do whatever else you have to do up here and get back to Florida as soon as you can. I want you there."

"What's the hurry, Justin? You just got here."

"There are other people looking for the necklace . . . and they're in Naples now. I called John and he's supposed to be getting to Mrs. Gauvin before these other people do."

"Who are they?"

"Russians. I assume they want the Czar's necklace back."

"That necklace belongs to me, Justin. My grandmother handed it down from my mother to me. The value is secondary. It's the sentimental value that makes me want it. Do you think we can find it?"

Justin had to digest that. This was a change in tune. Before she said she wanted it because of the value. Something didn't sit right.

"We're going to damn well try, Susan. I don't have to tell you that I'll do whatever it takes to locate it and deliver it back to you."

"I believe you. Justin, I think I'm falling in love with you. I don't know if that's good or bad."

Pow! Talk about a slap to the side of the head. Somebody pinch him.

"It's good, Susan. I've already fallen in love with you." He squeezed her hand. "Let's get to your place. I've got to leave for Naples as soon as possible. Maybe if we have time before my plane leaves . . . well, maybe we can . . ."

"Make love? Yes, Justin. I'd like that. I hope the plane doesn't leave for hours." She put her car into gear and pulled away from the curb.

Chapter Ten

The airline had two seats open and if he hurried, one could be his. The plane was scheduled to leave within the half hour. Justin drove Susan's car because it was faster than a taxi. No time for a romantic interlude. He weaved in and around traffic, keeping his fingers crossed the police wouldn't stop him.

Curb-side, he gave Susan a passionate kiss and rushed through the terminal. He could see them closing the door to the ramp. Wait. He had to make this flight. Whew! He made it. They allowed him to board. He placed a call to John to meet him at the baggage area of the Fort Myers airport. He laid his head back, peering out the window as the plane taxied for take-off. His abrupt departure from Susan left him frustrated and angry, but he smiled when he thought of Susan. She tried everything to keep him from leaving, including resorting to tears.

When he awoke the aircraft was in its landing pattern at Fort Myers. He had been sleeping for over two and a half hours.

John was waiting for him at baggage claim. "Nice to see you again, Justin, Long time no see," He lifted

Justin's bag from the carousel. It had been less than forty eight hours.

"I heard that you were a bit active up there in Revere," John said. "I got a call from the Revere department. It seems that Bucci guy got pretty beat up. Was that your work? You're a bad boy, Justin"

Justin slapped his friend on the back. "Well, I got what I went for, but I didn't do much more to Bucci that the Russians hadn't already done."

As they drove from the parking lot of the airport, John asked, "What sort of info did you come back with?"

"You can get back to the Revere department that Bucci killed Sterling Berns. He confessed to me that he strangled him. Of course that's off-the record, so they'll have to muscle him for their own confession. He also said that those two Russians are still after Rochelle Gauvin. They think she has the necklace and so do I. She's the key, if she's still alive and they haven't got to her yet."

"I have people on her. They haven't made a move on her yet. Stay away from her, Justin. Chambers doesn't want you anywhere near this. He wanted to make sure you understood. He doesn't care much for you. Maybe he has a hair up his ass because you were a cop and quit the force. A carnal sin in his mind— a cop is always a cop."

"Yeah, well . . . we'll see how things fall, John. You can tell him that I've been told, but between you and me . . . I'm going to do what I have to do. For Susan. Things are getting serious between us. I've never been affected by a woman like this. I know it's crazy, but there just might be a wedding in the near future."

John punched him in the arm. "You? Married? That'll be something to see. Ole' lover boy, stuck with one woman."

The forty-five minute drive from Ft. Myers to Naples on I-75 flew by. First stop . . . , to check on Rochelle. John pulled into the Gauvin driveway and was immediately confronted by two plain clothes police, weapons drawn. Recognizing John, they holstered their weapons.

Justin rang the doorbell and waited. No answer.

"Are you sure she's here?" he asked.

"Yeah, she's here. I told her not to answer the door or turn any lights on or off," John said. He rang the bell again, three short rings and one long ring.

The mini-blind on the sidelight moved slightly before Mrs. Gauvin opened the door. Justin and John walked in to see a distraught woman, wringing her hands.

"Have you caught them yet? My God, I don't want to die the way Richard did." She started to cry. "He was a cheating bastard, but I still loved him."

Justin took her by the elbow and led her into the living room. They sat on the sofa.

"Rochelle," Justin said, "Bucci told me he sent you the necklace. You signed for it. Your life is in danger. It's time to tell us the truth. Did you pass it to the buyer?"

"Let's understand each other," John said. "We can pull your police protection and let the Russians come for the necklace. They already tried it once when Justin intervened. They're not going to stop.

"I don't think you'd want them back here, not after seeing what they did to Bucci," said Justin.

"What did they do to him?" she asked, still sobbing.

"For starters, they pulled out some fingernails. That's not a very pleasant feeling, Rochelle. And they beat him quite badly."

"Justin, hold it," John said. "There's no need to scare her like this. Rochelle, the fact is, your husband's dead, Sterling Berns is dead and you could be next. You must tell us what you know."

Mrs. Gauvin looked up at them and said, "I know nothing about a necklace."

Damn it. Maybe they already got the necklace from her and let her live, with the threat they'd come back if she talked. But Justin doubted that. Why would they let her live? They had nothing to gain by that.

"Okay," Justin said. "Rochelle, if that's the way you want to play this, then that's how we'll play. Let's go, John. It's her call. I say, pull your men. Apparently she doesn't believe us."

John gave her one more chance. "Rochelle, I wish you luck. You're making a big mistake, but we can't protect you if you won't be honest with us. I'm pulling my men off the case."

They gave instructions for the two plain clothes police officers to abandon their post, but unbeknownst to Rochelle, they returned in more hidden locations to watch out for her.

John dropped Justin off at his condo, promising to keep him abreast of any situation.

What more could they do? They seemed no closer to finding the necklace than the beginning. The Russians had to have it. Justin doubted they would return it to the Kremlin, the rightful owners. Chances are these were thugs, EX-KGB and probably had their own buyer in the Soviet Union.

Justin's phone rang as he started to doze off. "Justin, please, come back to Boston. I need you."

Susan. What did she think, that he was made of money? He couldn't keep flying back and forth like it was nothing. "I'm sorry, Susan. I just got back. Things are starting to come together and I have to be here." *Well, not exactly together.* "I want to be with you too . . . please don't make it any harder than it already is."

The line went dead. What the fuck? Did she really hang up on him? Should he call her back? Women. He'd never understand them. Maybe she needed some time to cool off. Hell, he needed some time to cool off. Where does she get off ordering him around? He's not a God-damn millionaire. Besides, he had a job to do. A job she was paying him to do.

After John dropped Justin off, he drove back to the police station and picked up Detective Sandy Stracher. Her forte was working undercover. She wore a big floppy hat and an oversized jogging suit that put thirty pounds on her appearance. They pulled into the drive of the Gauvin home. Using the coded signal, they rang the bell. Rochelle checked to see that it was John Muldoon and opened the door. John and Sandy entered and shut the door behind them.

"Come with me." Sandy took Rochelle by the hand and let her to the bathroom. "Give me your robe," Sandy said.

"What are you doing?" Rochelle demanded.

"We are switching places. You're not safe here." Sandy peeled off the jogging clothes, exposing the layers of padding hiding her petite frame.

"I thought the police pulled all my protection. I thought I was on my own."

Sandy didn't answer, pointing to the jogging clothes on the floor. Rochelle picked them up and put them on. They were a little tight.

Sandy slipped on Rochelle's robe, which could have wrapped around her twice if it weren't for the padding. She felt something heavy in the pocket. Reaching in, she pulled out a .38 caliber hand gun. She checked the clip and put it back in the pocket.

"Just in case." Rochelle explained to her. "It was Richards"

Did Rochelle Gauvin even know how to shoot a gun? Rochelle dawned Sandy's big floppy hat and followed John to the squad car.

"Where are you taking me?" Rochelle asked.

He walked her briskly into the police station. "Rochelle, we're holding you in protective custody for a few days. Your life is in danger whether you believe it or not. We can't let you get yourself killed."

"This is preposterous. You can't hold me here, like a common criminal. I want to see the police chief . . . the man in charge."

"Tonight, I'm the man in charge."

Rochelle was led to a two-room lock-up, huffing with indignation the whole way. "Well, we'll see about this. I want to call my lawyer."

"You'll be quite comfortable here, and quite safe," John assured her. "Look, you're only getting in deeper and deeper. I can't protect you forever. I don't want to see you hurt."

She stood silent for a few moments.

"Okay, Sergeant. I'll tell you the truth. My husband and I made a deal with Bucci. He sent the necklace to us, like you said. We had it for a few days, waiting for things to cool down, then Richard was killed and the necklace disappeared while I was in Orlando. That's the truth, Sergeant. I don't know who has the necklace now. Whoever killed my husband, I guess."

"We'll try to make you comfortable. Just bear with us. We'll find those guys."
Her shoulders drooped and she looked resigned to the idea of staying in custody for now.

"Thank you, Sergeant. I appreciate what you're doing. I hope that policewoman doesn't get hurt pretending to me be. Sergeant . . . Will I be going to prison for being involved in this?"

"I can't answer that, Rochelle. Not until we see where all this leads. You're willingness to fill us in will go in your favor."

Right then John was hoping the Russians would come back to her house. If they already had the necklace, they'd have no reason to. If they didn't, they'd be back, and the police would be waiting for them.

"Have a good night, Rochelle. I'll drop in to see how you're doing in the morning. If you need or want just ask the officers on duty. They've been instructed to help you in any way they can."

"Thank you, Sergeant."

Chapter Eleven

Justin heard gunshots. He had to find cover. No, it wasn't gunfire. It was his phone ringing on the bed stand. His groggy brain disconnected the dream from reality. He reached for the phone, knocking it onto the floor.

"Damn," he said, as he fished around, feeling for the elusive receiver. "Hello?"

"Justin," Susan's voice said through the receiver. "I'm sorry I hung up on you last night. I miss you so much. I wanted you so bad last night. I still want you. Why won't you come back to me?"

He pulled himself to a sitting position, running a hand through his hair. "Susan, this is your case I'm working on. People have been killed. I can't just drop this. I want you just as bad, but I can't leave right now."

"Maybe I won't be here when you're ready, Justin. What if I fire you? Then you'd be free to come up here."

She wasn't making any sense. Were all women like this? Maybe he should let her fire him, and maybe he should run like hell from this crazy broad.

"What the hell's wrong with you, Susan? I'm trying to help you."

"Maybe I'll find somebody else to satisfy me today, Justin. You're not the only man that wants me, you know."

"Susan, look . . ." The line went dead. She hung up on him again. "Fuck."

As he dressed there was a knock on his door. So distracted thinking about Susan, he unlocked the door without checking who was there. The door flew in against him throwing him backwards, almost knocking him down. He caught himself and tried to reach the bedroom, where his gun was laying on his night table. An arm grabbed him around his neck and pulled him backwards and onto the floor. A second man stood over him with a gun pointing it at his head.

"Mr. Wade. I like your name. It reminds me of home. I worked in Wadi for over twenty years. You have heard of KGB, yes?"

"Yeah," Justin said, trying to loosen the grip around his throat. "I know the KGB. I believe we've already met. You sandbagged me at the travel agency." Boris chuckled. "Yes, sandbagged. I like this American term. This time, Mr. Wade, you will tell us what we want to know."

"Can I get up first?"

Boris laughed. "By all means. Oleg, tie his wrists."

"You don't have to do that. I won't cause any problems. We can talk," Justin said.

"Come now. I am not that naive. I am KGB. We are smarter than you Americans. Politics tore our country apart, not people like you. Now, let us get down to business. You know what I want . . . where is it?"

"How would I know where it is? It appears we are both on the same hunt."

"Where do you think it is?" Boris asked.

Justin shook his head. "I thought you had it. If not you, then I have no idea who has it, where it is or even exactly what *it* is. I've never seen what you are looking for, but I assume you mean the necklace called The Romanov Star. I know you hurt Ken Bucci, up in Boston. And I know that our meeting also puts my life in danger. I'm not stupid, either. But I can tell you this. The police know you're here and if you kill me you'll never leave Florida."

"Ah, see, I don't need to kill you, Mr. Wade. I just need to make sure you can't identify us to your police."

"What do you have in mind?" He had to think fast. If only he could distract the one doing the talking, he could take the other with one big head butt.

"Well . . ." His reply was cut short by the ringing of Justin's door bell. Boris and Oleg quickly moved to either side of Justin.

"Ask who it is," Boris whispered, with his gun pushed into Justin's neck.

"Who is it?" Justin yelled out.

"It's me, John. Open up."

Boris pressed the gun a little harder against his temple.

"Ah . . . I'm kinda tied up, John. Why don't you come back later?"

"I have to see you, Slick. Open the door."

"Damn it. I told you, I'm busy," Justin said, sounding annoyed. "I'll call you and Estelle later, when I'm through. Give me a break, Tucky. I'll get back to you." Would John get the encrypted message? There was silence on the other side of the door for a moment.

"Okay, Pal," John padded on the door with the palm of his hand. "I'll wait until I hear from you. Hey,

Slick. Whoever that broad is in there with you, give her one for me."

"Right, I will." Justin faked a laugh.

"Very good," Boris said. "You did well. Now, what shall we do with you? How am I going to get you off this case?"

"What threat am I to you? I'm already off the case. It's all in the hands of America's finest police officers now."

"The police we can handle. Americans are stupid. Do you think local police can get to us? They have to follow the law . . . you, on the other hand can do what you want. You are more dangerous to me than the police."

"Look," Justin said. "I told you. I'm off the case. Not only did the police take over the investigation, but my client fired me."

Just then the something crashed through the window and immediately filled the room with tear gas. Justin spun around and kicked Boris in the crotch. Boris doubled over and Justin smashed his knee into his face. Through tear-filled eyes Justin turned to Oleg. He was about to kick him in the stomach when the front door burst open and John, with his gun drawn threw himself to the floor and shot Oleg in the leg. Justin watched a figure dart through the fog out the front door. He staggered toward the doorway, his hands tied in front of him. His eyes were tearing so badly that he couldn't make out who it was. It felt like somebody had thrown a handful of sand in his eyes. He looked up and down the hallway but saw nothing. He looked back into the apartment to see John pulling Oleg out the front door. Two uniformed police officers came bursting through the stairwell exit doors, their weapons drawn.

"Did you see anybody come out of the building?" Justin asked them.

"Only a woman and a young boy." the one answered.

The corporal said, "You okay? Did the tear gas do the trick?"

"Yeah," Justin said. "Perfect. Thanks John. I was hoping you got the message."

"I guess I know you pretty well, Slick. Estelle and Tucky?" He put his head back and howled into the wind. "Was that the best you could come up with?"

"Remember that lady, Estelle, who tried to shoot me? Well, that son-of-a-bitch was about to complete her mission."

"And you thought I don't listen to you." John said.

"Get these tie-wraps off of me, John. I have to wash this shit out of my eyes. I haven't had tear gas in my face since I left the service. I screwed up during tear gas training and pulled my mask off too soon. I thought I was going blind. Your tear gas brought back some old, bad memories."

Oleg's eyes were so swollen from the tears that his faced looked contorted. The officers had him bound behind his back and he couldn't wipe them, a small blessing in disguise.

John and the uniformed officer took Oleg into custody while Justin went into the bathroom to clean his eyes. Then he called the condo association, informing of the situation and his promise to pay for all repairs. He finished dressing and joined John, who was waiting for him by his car.

Chapter Twelve

Boris walked through the lobby of the Holiday Inn, and went directly to the pay phones at the far end of the lobby. He placed a collect call to Helga, in Boston. "Helga, good morning. I hope I didn't wake you. I know it is late. This is Boris. I need your help. Can you come to Florida at great haste?"

"I . . . I suppose so. I can try to get a flight there by morning. What is it you need, Boris?"
He heard the hopefulness in her voice. "I need help with a business matter. I need somebody . . . a woman, to help me get to the person I'm after. Would you do that for me?"

"Yes, I suppose. Where shall I meet you, Boris?"

"I'm in Naples. You can fly direct into Fort Myers. I'll have a room ready for you here at the Holiday Inn Naples on Ninth Street, also called the Tamiami Trail. Take a taxi here. I'll be registered under the name I used in the old days. Do you remember, Helga?"

"Of course," she said. "How could I forget, Mr. Valentine?"

"Helga, perhaps this doesn't all have to be business. I would like very much to talk further on the subject we started last week."

"I'm looking forward to it, Boris."

"Wonderful. Thank you, Helga. Until tomorrow."

Boris checked in. One room. He'd be optimistic that the lovely Helga would share his room. Now about Oleg. Would he keep his mouth shut long enough for him to accomplish his plan? They didn't have any hard evidence on him. The most they could book him for was disorderly conduct. Welcome to America. In Russia, they didn't need solid evidence to hold someone. And their tactics to make somebody's tongue loose were primitive, but very effective. He knew that Oleg was aware that if things went well, he'd get his share of whatever Boris was rewarded. He wouldn't talk. Boris checked out of his other hotel and slowly drove back to the Holiday Inn. He unpacked, walked across the street for a hamburger and beer and took two more sandwiches to go. He pulled the heavy black-out curtains across the windows.

He awakened before dawn, looked at the alarm clock, rolled over and went back to sleep. When next he awoke, it was to a knock on the door. The clock confirmed his thoughts. Shit. He'd spent most of the day in bed. He pulled his gun from beneath his pillow, switched the light out, and walked silently to the side of the door.

"Who is it?"

"Mr. Valentine, please open the door."

Helga. Boris held the gun steady as he unlocked the door to let her slip through a partially opened door. She looked at the gun without saying anything and met his stare. Boris lowered the gun and dropped it on the side table. He could feel the heat from her body, smell the musky scent of body wash or shampoo. They stood facing each other, their bodies inches apart.

"Helga," he finally spoke. "I'm so happy to see you. I've been thinking about you all week."

"Boris, they didn't have reservation for me downstairs under my code name. So I asked for Mr. Valentine's room." She blushed and lowered her eyes. "I told the clerk I was your girlfriend and wanted to surprise you. Should I get a room of my own?"

Her eyes already told him that she didn't want to. "I was hoping we could stay together. Is that all right?"

"Of course . . . Mr. Valentine. I'd like that very much."

His manhood was evident under the thin cotton pajamas he still wore. "We are both a little older, Helga, but you are more beautiful than ever. I was very foolish to let you get away and marry Igor."

"Yes, you were, Boris. It was you that I always wanted. But, I am here now."

Boris circled his arms around her waist and drew her near. They kissed softly. Helga slipped her tongue into Boris' mouth. He tasted her and groaned. It had been too long since he had a woman. He must slow things down.

"Helga. It's been too long for me. I'm afraid I cannot contain myself."

Helga nodded, pulled out of his arms and retrieved her bag, exiting from the room into the bathroom.

Boris quickly gulped some Vodka to wash the taste of sleep from his mouth, stripped naked and slid back under the still-warm covers.

Helga appeared in the doorway of the lighted bathroom in a black, skimpy nightie. The light from the bathroom left little to his imagination. The V between her legs was bushy. She clicked off the bathroom light and found her way to the bed in the darkness.

He pulled her on top of him, his hardness pressed tight against her belly. She kissed his lips, his chin his neck. She moved slowly down him, kissing his hairy chest, his erect nipple, his navel.

She took his manhood in her hand, gently stroking it. Boris strained to keep from exploding. She sat up and straddled him, slipping his penis into her. On the second stroke Helga moaned. He was in as deep as he could go. She, with quick, short movements tipped him over the edge. He burst inside her. Even as he climbed down from that mountain of ecstasy, his hardness was slow to fade. Helga continued thrusting until she gasped and the shuddered with satisfaction of her own.

"Oh, my," she said. "Oh, my," she repeated several more times.
Boris began to slide her off his body, but she cuddled her neck into his.

"Nyet," she said, "No hurry. I want to savor this and never forget how this feels."

Me too. "Give me a few minutes, my love. We will have more to remember."

"Oh yes, Boris. Many more to remember, from tonight."
They lay in each other's arms with Helga's face in his neck, nibbling and kissing him. Boris reached down and felt her still hot and wet triangle of hair. She started moving her hips in unison with his fingers. As his pace picked up, her hips rose up to meet his fingers, faster and faster.

Boris felt his hardness returning and slid himself into her as she engulfed him with her legs, pulling him with each thrust. There was no way he could hold his erection this soon since his last climax. But he wanted too. Oh, how he wanted to. He raised himself off her body, and remained on his hands and knees letting her move wildly under him.

"Boris, Boris," she cried as they reached their climax together. When his heart rate began to return to normal, he rolled over and they lay again in each other's arms. Exhausted and spent, they both dozed off.

Boris was awakened by the feel of something between his legs. He opened his eyes and in the darkened room he could see the top of Helga's head. He reached down and rubbed her cheek affectionately. He grasped the sheets on both sides of the bed as he let her lead him again to that special place.

She was a tiger in bed. Why had he ever let Igor have her? What a fool he had been. She slipped from the bed and headed for the bathroom. She paused just long enough in the light of the bathroom for him to enjoy the beauty of her naked body.

By the time Helga finished showering, Boris looked through the black-out curtains to see the last of daylight slipping away again. They had lost an entire day in bed. But what a day.

She sat on the edge of the bed. "So, Mr. Valentine. Why am I here? Besides to bed me . . . you have a job for me to do, yes?"

"Yes, my beautiful lover. I have a job for you. But rest assured . . . I was going back to Boston to see you when this job was finished. That is exactly true, Helga."

"I believe you, Boris"

Boris smiled at her and pulled her down to him. He slipped her robe off and they made love one more time before they both drifted off to sleep.

They made love one more time in the morning before taking turns in the shower. Boris watched her as she dressed. He felt himself getting hard again. No, he must wait to have his hands all over her again. She was insatiable. They had to find something else to do outside of the bedroom until darkness set in. They decided to take a tour through the Everglades in an air boat to see the alligators, Florida panthers, and the wild coast of Florida. They returned from their long, hot and humid day, to the coolness of their room. After quick shower to wash the away the sweat from a day in the Everglades, they enjoyed a quiet dinner at the Pacific 41 restaurant, as the sun was going down. They returned to the room to discuss their plan in private.

Helga looked at her watch then went to the window. "It's dark out, Boris. I think it is dark enough."

Boris came up behind her and peeked through the drapes.

"Yes, let us go now."

Chapter Thirteen

It was eleven o'clock in the morning when John drove to the Gauvin home with Rochelle in tow. There had been no news all night from the officers. Perhaps he was wrong about his hunch they would come back. She wanted to go home and there was nothing he could do to stop her.

The undercover police nodded as they made their way to the front door. Rochelle used her key to enter. Where was Sandy?

They heard muffled cries from the bedroom. John told Rochelle to stay put, as he drew his weapon and headed for the bedroom. Sandy was tied to the bedpost, her mouth covered with duct tape. He placed a finger to lips to silence her and did a quick sweep of the room for other occupants. Finding no one, he quickly untied her and ripped the tape off her mouth as gently as he could.

"What happened Sandy? Are you okay?"

She had a nasty bruise on her face. "I'm fine. A woman came to the door. She claimed to be an ex-lover of Richard Gauvin. She wanted to confess the whole story to his wife. I tried to tell her I wasn't interested in what my husband had done, that it was too late now since he was dead.

"Before I could shut the door, she forced her foot in, and then I was grabbed from behind . . . one hand over my mouth and the other twisting my arm behind me. A man dragged me away from the front door. My gun fell from the pocket of the bathrobe.

"They recognized it as a police weapon. The woman called the man, Mr. Valentine."

"They could have killed you," John said. "How did he get in? "Where were the agents while this happened?" John glared at the officer standing in the doorway.

"Not his fault," Sandy said. "I let her in. Stupid mistake. I thought I could handle her. We had a code word if I needed help. I didn't give it to him. He stood his post outside. The other was still in the car, down a block watching from the street."

Rochelle called out from the other room. "Sergeant, the back door lock is broken and the screen is ripped from the screen door. Is everything okay in there?"

"You can come in, Rochelle. Sandy is fine." He turned toward his officer. "You are fine, right, Sandy?"

"Yes, and relieved you're here. They wanted to know where the necklace was."

"Can you describe them?"

"Foreign, Russian or Romanian. They bragged about being KGB. Then the man realized that I wasn't Rochelle Gauvin. He said he had seen her before at the travel agency. They knew I was an undercover cop. That's when he hit me." She rubbed her swollen cheek.

"One more person to add to the puzzle." He turned to Rochelle. "I really don't think it's wise for you to stay here. We can put you in a safe house so you don't have to stay at the station.

Justin devoured his third cup of coffee at Bad Boys restaurant when his cell phone rang. It was John, calling from the Gauvin house. So much for a quiet breakfast. Justin paid the server and headed straight over. A uniformed police officer was waiting at the open front door as he pulled into the driveway.

Justin rushed into the house. The undercover was rubbing her wrists where the tie straps had cut into them. She repeated the story to him. There was something about this woman that Justin liked. She was tough, but didn't look it. And she didn't cast blame on anyone else for her mistakes. He liked that, too.

"You're very lucky," John said. "I'm beginning to think these guys are not our killers. They didn't kill Rochelle or Justin when they had the chance, and they didn't kill you. If Bucci killed Sterling Berns, somebody else must have killed Richard Gauvin. There's someone else besides the Russians looking for this necklace . . . and I think he's Gauvin's killer."

Rochelle insisted on staying in her house. The best they could do was place an extra guard at the back door.

"If you have nothing to add, Mrs. Gauvin, we will leave you in these men's care. And Officer Stuart, try to stay alert to any unusual activity."

"Yes sir, I will surely do that."

As they drove back to the station John said it was times like this he wished he wasn't bound by the law. "I'd like to take that Russian into a back room and find out what he knows. Unfortunately, Justin, I can't do that."

Justin stoked his chin, sinister like. "But— if by some means you turned your back, someone else might be able to muscle some information out of him."

"I can't do that, Justin. Besides, there could be international complications and that would be another bag of worms.

If only he could provoke Oleg to pick a fight with him, outside of the station. They needed something to hold him, or he would walk scot free.

Lieutenant Chambers was waiting as they entered the police station together. "What the hell are you doing, Muldoon? This case is a major fuck-up. Sandy gets mugged while two uniformed officers pick their noses outside? And where are you during all this? Having coffee?"

"Screw you, Lieutenant," John responded. "Get off my ass! This is my case and I'll handle it."

"You wait here," he said to Justin as he walked into the holding cells. He returned a few minutes later with Oleg in tow. "Release him," he said to the booking clerk.

John turned to Oleg. "I suggest you keep your nose clean. And try not to get into any street brawls or I'll have to haul your ass back in here." He winked at Justin.

Oleg glared at him. "What are you talking about?"

Justin really wanted to get even with this bastard for their last encounter. And he wanted to solve the mystery of the necklace.

Oleg tugged at his jacket. "See, you can't hold me. I'm a tourist on vacation and you have mistreated me. I'll file a complaint with . . ."

John interrupted his discourse by pushing him against the wall. "Listen, you Russian bastard. You think you can come into this country and mess our citizens up. Not in my town, you can't."

Justin smiled to himself. John sounded like a sheriff from a bad western movie. He followed Oleg out the door. He tailed close behind him, making sure Oleg knew he was being followed. Oleg ducked into a bar. Justin sat on the stool right next to him. Oleg headed for the men's room. Suddenly, Justin needed to take a piss.

They didn't speak, but even when Oleg hailed a cab and went to the Sea Shell Motel on 9th Ave. Justin was close on his tail. *Come on, get pissed off. Start something.*

As Oleg exited the cab, Justin exited his El Dorado. Oleg spun on his heels. "Stop following me!"

"It's a free country man," Justin said. "Did you forget where you are?"

"What do you want from me?" Oleg asked, spittle forming in the corner of his lips.

"Well, Mr. Oleg Popov, I'm not the police, as you know. I'm the guy you knocked on the head in Mrs. Gauvins travel agency. Do you . . ."

"You stupid Americans. Do you think you can scare a Russian? You are garbage."

That's it. He smashed Oleg on the side of his jaw. Oleg crashed against the building and slid to the pavement floor. Justin lifted him by the shirt, and forced his head against the siding.

"Do you really think I'm weak, Mr. Popov?" He dug his fist into Oleg's midsection, doubling him over, forcing him to throw up on Justin's shoe.

"You son-of-a-bitch," Justin said. He removed his shoe and wiped it across Oleg's face, and then banged his head back against the wall, just for good measure.

"Is your partner in here?" Oleg spat the blood from his mouth onto Justin's shirt.

This bastard was tough. He had to give him that. Justin looked down at his shirt. "You really shouldn't have done that" He smashed his fist into Oleg's face, breaking his nose. Blood spurt out in all directions as Justin's left hook caught Oleg on the other side of his face at eye level.

Oleg's eyes rolled back as he slumped to the ground. Justin towered over the crumbled, broken man.

"Now, where is your partner? Here? Which room? I can bust down every door, but it's only going to mess up your pretty face some more. Oleg mumbled something that Justin couldn't understand.

"Say again?" Oleg mumbled through a mouth full of broken teeth and blood, "Rzzz . . . da Rzzz Carlton"

"Under what name?"

"Smith, John Smith"

Justin laughed. Very original. "Smith, huh? What's his real name?"

"Lushin, Boris Lushin."

Justin pulled him back to his feet. "What's the name of the woman he's working with?"

Blood poured from Oleg's broken nose and spat a mouth full of blood on the ground.

"I don't know any woman with him."

Justin brought his fist back, as if he was going to hit Oleg again.

"Don't . . . I don't know!" Oleg said, as he started to sob.

Who were the weak Americans now? Justin let go of his shirt and Oleg slumped back to the ground.

He roared the engine of the El Dorado and hit the speed dial on his cell for John.

"The other Russian's at the Ritz. Under the name of John Smith." The false name won't do any good, but their security cameras should spot the guy. Justin could identify him. He'd never forget that face when they met at the travel agency when they threatened Rochelle.

Chapter Fourteen

As Justin exited his car, he looked up at the window of his apartment. He stopped short. There were lights on, lights that he knew he hadn't left on. He exited the elevator one floor above his and walked down the flight with his gun drawn. He poked his head through the slightly opened door of the stairwell. Nothing. He slid against the hallway wall until he came to his door and quietly slipped his key into the lock, gently turned the key and opened the door slowly and quietly snuck through. He left the door open and worked his way through the short entrance way until he could see the entire living room area. Clear. He heard a noise in his bedroom. Adrenalin coursed through his veins. He sighed deeply, making sure his pistol was off safety and barged through the bedroom door, dropping to the floor and aiming the gun at the person standing beside his bed.

"Ahhh!" A woman's scream stopped him from shooting. Susan.

"Jesus Christ! I could've shot you. Why didn't you tell me you would be here?" Damn, that was a stupid thing for her to do. Especially now with everything that was happening.

Susan, stammered. "I . . . I'm sorry, Justin. I thought I'd surprise you."

"How did you get in here," Justin asked.

"The president of your association saw us together before and he let me in so I wouldn't have to wait outside in the heat. Aren't you glad to see me?"

"Of course I'm glad to see you. I wasn't sure how things stood after you hung up on me, twice." But he would definitely have a talk with that association president. He couldn't be letting people into condos, just because he saw them together. Did they really vote that idiot into office? Maybe he would have to start attending those damn owners meetings.

"I'm sorry about that, Justin. I wanted you up in Boston with me."

Boy, this broad really was a rich, stuck-up little bitch, wasn't she? Was he supposed to come running like a dog in heat whenever she snapped her fingers?

She moved close enough to him that he could smell her perfume. "Aren't you going to kiss me hello?"

He backtracked and shut the door. "I'm afraid my heart wouldn't be in it, right now. My hearts racing a mile a minute, and it's not romance. I thought you were one of those Russians."

"The Russians have been after you?" Susan asked.

"Yeah. They are getting desperate. Obviously, they don't have the necklace and they are chasing the same trails as I am, looking for it. But, don't worry, I'll find it."

"Why don't we just forget about the necklace, Justin? You and I can just go away. We could live in Europe or even in the Caribbean. Anyplace you want, Justin. Come away with me, let the Russians have the necklace." She tried to move into his embrace.

"Are you crazy? That necklace is worth over fifteen million. You can't be serious about walking away from that kind of money."

"I don't care about the money, Justin. I care about you." Her perfume was intoxicating. She brushed her lips against his. "It would be like a honeymoon for us. Doesn't that mean anything to you?"

Justin wasn't sure if it was her musky scent, or the warmth radiating from her body, pressed close against him. He couldn't think straight. "Um, it sounds great, Susan, but…"

She nibbled on his ear. "We could leave first thing in the morning. Say yes, Justin."
He backed away, trying to clear his head. "Let me think about it. Are you implying that I should live off your money my whole life?"

"Why not? I have enough for both of us. But if you really wanted to work, that would be up to you. We could even get married, if you want me."

Justin knew he was falling in love with her. But married? Living off a woman? Not his style at all. And this sudden lack of interest in the necklace made no sense.

"Give me time to think about it, Susan. That's a big step for me." He let her move back into his arms. Damn she felt good.

"Okay, sweetheart. We'll talk more in the morning. I could use a shower right now. Am I staying here tonight," she asked.

"You are staying here, unless you *want* to get a hotel room."

"Of course not. I just wanted to hear you say it. I want to make love with you tonight, Justin. Not love *to you*, but love *with you*." She kissed him, long and hard, her tongue slowly finding its way between his lips.

Justin could feel himself getting hard. He broke away from her and patted her on the behind, "Get into that shower, Susan. I think I'm more than ready for you."

She reached down and grasped his bulging member through his pants. Her eyes twinkled with mischief and she started to un-zipper his pants.

He groaned. "After our showers, Susan. I've been sweating all day and I don't want to put anything into you that isn't clean. Especially that beautiful mouth of yours."

"Ooh," she said, "Are you going to let me put that hard thing . . ."

Justin stopped her in mid-sentence. "Yes, I'm going to let you," he said, smiling.

Susan did a slow strip-tease in front of him, and disappeared into the bathroom. He sat on the edge of the bed, unconsciously stroking his member, imagining what it would be like to be to be married to her. They could live like a king and queen in some of those counties, servants, groundskeepers, everything at his fingertips. Did she really have that much money that she could walk away from fifteen million? Or was she really that non-materialistic, that it really didn't matter to her? He shook his head, not knowing what to do. This was something men only dreamed about and it had fallen into his lap. He lay back on the bed, smiling.

Susan walked into the bedroom, nude. The bedroom was dark, but the bathroom light behind cast a frame around her. God she was beautiful. She approached the bed and once again attempted to unzip his pants. This time, he didn't stop her. She reached in and gently withdrew his penis and held it in her hands. Before she could go down on him, he pulled her up to him and they kissed softly. To hell with his shower. He couldn't wait. The heat between them rose. She straddled him and guided his penis into her sweet spot. The bathroom light cast the perfect glow, and he could watch her expression as she rode him to climax. They made love three more times before drifting off into a well-deserved sleep.

Morning came too soon as the day peeked through the uncovered bedroom window. Justin stretched. He could still taste her. He slid out of bed and slipped into the shower without waking Susan. He emerged with a towel wrapped around his waist to find Susan standing in front of the window, nude, staring at the lake that surrounded his condo. She had the body of a twenty-year-old in spite of her forty years. She turned and faced him. Her tight erect breasts beckoned him to take her back to bed. As she turned to him, he wondered how she could still have the tight, firm breasts of a twenty year old.

"Get into the shower," he said. "I have things to do and you can come along. Unless, of course, you have something else to do?"

"I thought we were going to make arrangements to go away today." Her lips tuned into a pout.

"Hell, Susan, we can't just up and leave. We can make arrangements, maybe, but there are things I'd have to do beforehand. There's this condo, my business, your case, my friends, too much to do on such short notice. We can make plans to go, maybe in a few weeks."

Susan stomped her foot. "A few weeks! No, I want to go right away, not in a few weeks. I'll wait two or three days, but I won't wait a week. You better decide what you want; me and a life of luxury or this terrible business of yours in this God forsaken Florida. Make up your mind, Justin. You can't have us both." She dressed in a fury and left the apartment.

What the fuck? He turned and walked into the bathroom. He angrily went through his morning routine, dropping the bar of soap twice in the shower, cutting himself shaving, and left the condo, confused and talking to himself. He drove to John Muldoon's home and laid the situation out for John and Dorothy.

"What is keeping you here?" John asked.

"My business, my friends . . . you."

They echoed what he had been thinking last night, an offer like this doesn't come around every day. They also felt that if he was in love with her, by all means, he should marry her.

"I don't know, Toody," Justin said. "Sometimes she shows a side of herself that scares me. When she gets angry, for no particular reason, she shows an ugly side of herself."

John punched him in the arm.

"Yea, and you're always such a gem to be around. I don't know what to tell you, Justin. Most women, when they get angry, have a mean side to them," John flinched as Dorothy's fist landed against his arm. "See what I mean, Slick?"

"Sweetheart, listen to me," Dorothy said. "If you love her, and you marry her there'll always be spats between you. But you work through them. Besides, things will probably get calmer once you are married. It sounds like all she wants is you, what's wrong with that? Not everyone gets an opportunity to live in the lap of luxury the rest of their lives. Do you want to live on love, in poverty, as John and I are doing?" She looked at John with nothing but love in her eyes.

"Jesus, you two," Justin said, shaking his head. "What I need is a lady like you, Dorothy. Then I wouldn't think twice about it."

"That's nice to hear, Justin. I feel the same about John. We have a good, loving relationship. It's been this way for over fifteen years." She leaned over and kissed John on the cheek.

"Well, I have to make my mind up pretty soon," Justin said. "She's really pushing me. She wants to forget about the necklace and just go away . . . today."

John frowned. "You didn't mention that part. She wants to forget about the necklace, Justin? Why would she walk away from fifteen million dollars?"

"That's it Toody, I don't know. She claims she has all the money she needs . . . enough to last the rest of our lives."

John shook his head. "Still . . . fifteen million dollars. As a cop, that can't help but shoot off about fifteen million red flags"

"I know. It certainly does sound crazy. By the way, did you find out anything at the Ritz?"

"Nothing. We pulled the security tape from the front desk and compared each person with the time they signed in. Nothing matches and none of the bellhops remember a thing. Not even somebody that spoke with a Russian accent."

"How are you coming with the investigation of Mr. Gauvin? Anything at all?" Justin asked.

"That's a dead end, so far. It was made to look like the Mafia, but we know it wasn't. Somebody searched their house, or at least one room, which possibly means who-ever did the searching found what they were looking for right away. Otherwise they would have gone through more rooms than one."

Justin nodded. "That's the way it sounds. But who the hell could have done it? We've gone through just about everybody who's involved in any way."

"It's beyond me, Slick," John said.

"What about the insurance money for the necklace. Has anybody checked that out? Has Susan already received the funds?" He wasn't liking the feeling that was crawling up from his gut.

"Hell, Justin. One of the other officers were supposed to check on that, but it skipped my mind. I guess I'm getting too close to this case with you involved. Lieutenant Chambers is up my ass about it. If I didn't know better I would think that *he* was involved somehow. He's never been such a hard-ass over any case I've had before."

"Toody, you've got to stop watching those cop shows. You're getting paranoid. Do you want me to tail the Lieutenant?"

John laughed. "No, you're right. I'm just paranoid, and a little pissed off that I haven't been able to solve this yet."

"Okay, John. Let me ask Susan about the insurance money on the necklace, if she's still speaking to me. She left my place in quite a huff this morning." He pulled his cell phone from his pocket. "Let me see if I can reach her now." He dialed her cell number and waited.

No answer and the recording said her voice mail was full and not accepting any more messages. Who was she talking to so much that her messages were full? Certainly not him.

"I'm going to see if I can track her down." He leaned over and gave Dorothy a peck on the cheek. "John, I'll get back to you at the station, later."

Relying on a hunch, he drove to Gauvin's travel agency. He spotted Susan through the plate glass window, standing in the lobby, looking through pamphlets. He parked and joined her.

"Is that where we're going?" he said, pointing over her shoulder at the pamphlet that said Spain.

She turned with a smile, but the warmth did not meet her eyes. "Only if we leave in a few days, sweetheart. Otherwise it'll be a ticket for one."

Justin ran his fingers through his brown hair. "I told you; I need some time, Susan."

"I heard you, Justin. Did you hear me?"

Justin looked at Rochelle Gauvin, watching the conversation between them without interrupting. "Can we take this conversation someplace else, Susan? I need some answers from you before I can give you an answer."

Susan slapped the pamphlet back on the counter, causing Rochelle to jump.

"Very well, lunch. You can buy me lunch." She sauntered out of the building in front of him.

Still a great ass. He hurried ahead of her to hold the car door to his El Dorado

They settled on Jacks River Bar on North Rd. Justin ordered their specialty burger, Jack's Double Trouble and Susan chose the chicken nachos. Justin waited until the server had left them alone. "Susan, I'm sorry to have to ask, but John needs the name of your insurance company for the necklace."

"Why?" She snapped back at him. "I don't want to hear anything more about that necklace. The insurance company is Prudential, in Boston. Tell John to drop the case." She crossed her arms across her chest.

"He can't do that Susan. There are two murders involved here even without finding the necklace. Susan, that's one of the reasons I haven't made my mind up yet. Sometimes you scare me with your mean streak. I don't know if I want to put up with that the rest of my life.

Especially with you footing all the bills. I wouldn't want you holding that over my head."

Her eyes softened and she relaxed her arms.

"Oh, Justin. I'm so sorry. I've been handling this very badly. Really, I don't have a mean bone in my body and I certainly don't want to treat you that way. It wouldn't be that way. I promise." Susan leaned across the table, giving him an amble view down her shirt.

"I love you, Justin. I want to be with you always and I promise to be a loving wife, if you'll have me."

The tightness in Justin's jeans seemed to be doing all the talking.

"Give me a couple of days, Let me close my personal business, here in Naples. If you want to forget about the necklace, that's your business. I can leave the investigation to John and the police department."

"That right. Let them earn their money. Let them look for the damn necklace. It has caused me nothing but trouble and heartache. I have a feeling that it's back in Russia by now anyway, don't you?"

"Possibly," Justin said. *Then why are the Russians still hunting for it?*

"Let's eat. I'm starving." Justin said, eyeing the huge burger placed in front of him.

"And afterwards?" That sparkle he loved was back in her eye.

"I know just the place," Justin replied. "Someplace quiet and dark. How's that sound?"

The television in Justin's bedroom lit the room as Susan rolled off of him. She pulled the sheet up to cover her nakedness. He rolled over and kissed her, before grabbing his cell phone and stepping naked into the kitchen.

"Come right back," she whispered.

"Toody, I wanted to tell you that the insurance company that's handling . . ."

John interrupted his message. "Yes, I know, Justin. I've been trying to locate you for a few hours. Why don't you keep your cell phone on? The Revere Police department faxed over the report. It's the Prudential, right?"

"Yep. That's it. What did you find out?"

"I'm not sure you're going to like this, Justin. Well, it seems that Susan filed a claim for the insurance money, and get this, Slick, the necklace was insured for twenty two million, not fifteen big ones. I guess she was covering the other pieces as well. The insurance company isn't ready to pay out that kind of loot. They are doing their own investigation. They'll probably fight the claim. The necklace and other jewelry was supposed to be kept in a safe deposit box. They haven't told Susan yet, that they may not pay up. I'd hate to be around her when she finds out."

"She's here with me now, John. I guess I'm the one that has to break the news to her. Unless, of course, you want to tell her."

"Oh no, I don't think so, Justin. I think you should be the one. Why should I have her hate me? Or . . . you could play dumb until the insurance company tells her."

She must have been expecting the money soon and that is what she planned to *retire* on. This definitely was going to upset her plans.

Justin walked into the bedroom where she was waiting for him. As he neared the bed, she reached out and grabbed his penis and gently pulled him to her, laughing at the way he yelped. She let him go and pulled him down on to the bed, wrapping her arms around his neck, planting a passionate kiss on his lips.

Justin shrank back and faced her. "Susan, I have to tell you something. I just spoke to John. Prudential called him about the necklace. They told him about your insurance claim."

Her face darkened and she pulled the sheet over her naked breasts. "Yes, so?"

"They're going to fight your claim. They told John you were supposed to keep the jewelry in a safe deposit box. They could tie up the process for years."

"Damn," she spat, jumping from the bed. She stomped naked into the bathroom, slamming the door behind her. *Crash!* Something smashed against the bathroom wall. He could hear her swearing, venomous words most distinguishable.

When the bathroom became quiet. Justin slipped his boxers on and knocked on the door. "Susan, may I come in?" He jiggled the handle and the door swung open. "I thought you didn't care about the necklace, or the money. Now, all of a sudden it's a big deal?"

"Of course it's big deal, you idiot. What the hell do you know? You're just a small town private detective. What do you know of three million dollars?"

"Wait a minute, wait a minute. Three Million? You filed a claim for twenty-two million. What's going on, Susan?"

"Nothing," she said as she breezed by Justin, heading to the bedroom. She quickly dressed, shot him a hateful look and stormed out of the condo. He watched her leave from his window as she flagged down one of his neighbors. After a few minutes, she got in his car and they drove away.

Justin placed another call to John. "That didn't go well, my friend. I just watched a beautiful woman become very ugly. There's something going on that I don't understand."

Where did she go? She didn't take anything but her purse. Her overnight bag still sat on his chair. Would there be any clues to it in there? He fingered the handle. Real Italian leather, not the pleather or cloth travel bags he used. No, he wasn't that kind of person. He didn't go through his girlfriend's things. A pesky needle ached at his side. You *are* a private detective. Was the head between his legs taking precedent over the one on his shoulders? He gave in and sat the bag on the bed. Tentatively he unzipped it and looked in. A make-up bag with the Gucci logo all over it. A sheer black nightie. Hmm. She never got a chance to wear it, more inclined to stay in the buff. A pair of black satin panties and matching lace bra. This was silly, and rude, a total invasion of privacy. How would she react if she walked through the door and found him snooping through her things? There was nothing in there but personal belonging. He zipped it shut, breathing a sigh of relief he wasn't caught with his fingers in the cookie jar.

Sleep eluded him and he finally gave in and took a sleeping pill. His sleep was restless and fraught with visons of living on a secluded island with Susan, then finding them both behind bars, trying to persuade whoever was interrogating them that he knew nothing about the whereabouts of the Romanov Star.

His cell phone rang, the irritating ring tone of the James Bond theme. "Damn, this is why I turn off this damn thing off."

"Justin, this is Susan." She didn't have to tell him, he recognized her voice immediately, and it didn't sound friendly. "Would you put my things outside your door? I'll pick them up momentarily."

He looked at the alarm clock by the bed. It said six a.m.

"Susan, where did you sleep last night?"

"That's none of your business. I did what I had to do."

Whoa. Where is this coming from? "What are you saying? Did you sleep with somebody?"

"I did what I had to do. Will you put my things out or not?" she said.

He felt his anger rising. Needles prickled at the back of his neck. "No, I won't put them out. You'll come in here for them like an adult. What the hell has gotten into you?"

"Look, it is over. You go back to your little detective business, and I'll go back to Boston. Just put my things out. I don't even want to look at you again."

"And what about, run away with me, I'll love you forever, let's get married? Was that all bull-shit?"

"Of course. You don't think I'd really want somebody like you?"

Justin exploded. He leaped from the bed, grabbed her damn leather bag and tossed it out the door into the hallway. Let someone steal it. It would serve her right. On second thought, make her come and beg for it. He dragged her bag back inside. "You're right, Susan. Why would you want somebody like me? Thank God I didn't jump on your offer to go away with you. You would have stranded me in some foreign country."

"Absolutely, I had my reasons."

"What are those, Susan?"

"Never mind. I've already said too much" The line went dead.

Justin hit the speed dial and called John. "Hey man. Sorry to call so early. I'm not positive, but I'm beginning to think Susan may be involved, after all. Can we get together and talk?"

"I can't, Justin. I have to meet with the Mayor and Lieutenant Chambers. They're both on my ass. Whatever you have to do, you'll have to do it by yourself. Do you need another officer to come over?"

"No, never mind. I'll handle it."

Justin heard a car door slam and looked out of the window. Susan and a big muscular man headed for the entrance to the building.

"Shit," Justin mumbled. "This looks like trouble."

Justin was putting on his jeans when he heard them in the hallway. Common sense told him to stay inside, behind a lock door. But since when did he use common sense? He had to face her.

"Where are my things? I told you to put them in the hall." Susan snapped at him.

"Oh! I see. I'll guess this is who you slept with last night, huh? Too bad you didn't have your slutty little lingerie." The minute it was out of his mouth, he regretted it.

Her eyes got wide. "You went through my things. How dare you!"

"I was looking for a next of kin in case this goon killed you. Thank you very much." That wasn't exactly true, but it was the first thing he could think of.

Superman moved in, his chest inches from Justine's head. He sucker-punched his gigantic fist against the side of Justin's head. Justin tumbled backwards, through the open doorway and landed on the living room sofa. Superman was standing over him before he could get up. Justin swung his foot up catching

Superman in the groin. While he was doubled over Justin again shot his foot out and caught Superman on the side of his jaw, knocking him down. Justin saw a flash out of the corner of his eye and ducked when Susan hurled an ash tray that smashed against the wall. He rose quickly and with all his might smashed Superman between his ear and his eye. No one should be able to get up from a tactic like that, but the behemoth shook it off and lunged at Justin again. Justin kicked him in the groin again, which doubled the giant over and gave Justin time to survey where and what Susan was up to. She rushed him, her fingernails raking across his face. He could feel the welts raising on his cheeks instantly. He pushed her away and she tripped over Superman, who was grabbing his crotch and throwing up all over his carpet. She toppled backwards and landed on her behind, legs in the air. He was too old for this shit. He grabbed Susan by the arm and dragged her out into the hall. Before Superman could get his wind back, Justin gave a swift kick and rolled him out into the hall was well.

Justin quickly shut the door and swiped the deadbolt across the door. He made a call to the police station and explained there were two people in his hallway. He said they were trying to break in, but he fended them off.

"We'll send a cruiser right over," the dispatcher said. "Are you hurt? Are the suspects armed?"

Maybe with 200 pounds of muscle, but Justin didn't see any weapons. Was Sergeant Muldoon available? He was a personal friend. The dispatcher said she would relay the information.

While he was waiting for the police to arrive, he heard movement outside his door. Through the peep hole, he saw Superman stand up into view. By the time John and a uniformed officer arrived, Superman and Susan were gone. Justin filled them in on everything. Did he want to press charges? No, but Susan's actions certainly pointed to something that wasn't kosher.

It didn't take long for the police to pick up Superman by Justin's description and the color and make of his car. They wouldn't be able to hold them unless he pressed charges or they found something else. John called Justin and told him to come down to the station.

John and Lieutenant Chambers were waiting as Justin walked into the police station. John reached Justin before he had an opportunity to say anything to the Lieutenant.

"Justin, for everybody's sake, keep your mouth shut. Don't volunteer your opinion on anything." John said.

"No problem, John. I won't embarrass you," Justin replied, with a big grin on his face.

Justin walked to Lieutenant Chambers with his hand extended. "I appreciate your letting me sit in, Lieutenant. I promise not to get in your way."

Lieutenant Chambers nodded to a uniformed officer, "Let's do it," he said.

The three of them were waiting in a small room, bare except for five chairs and a heavy metallic table, when the uniformed officer brought Susan into the room. She looked disheveled. Did he do that by pushing her down over the goon?

Lieutenant Chambers pulled a chair out for her. She sat heavily. Justin and Sergeant Muldoon took their seats as Lieutenant Chambers started the interrogation.

"Mrs. Berns, I'm Lieutenant Chambers. You already know Sergeant Muldoon and Justin Wade. I'm going to ask you a few questions. I'd appreciate honest answers. You're only here for questioning, you are not under arrest. Is all this clear?"

"Nobody's read me my rights, Lieutenant," she said, icily.

"That won't be necessary. As I said, you are not under arrest, Mrs. Berns."
She glared at Justin "Then I don't have to tell you anything."

"If you prefer, we can arrest you on suspicion," John said.

"Does *he* have to be here?" Her glare bore into Justin's soul. Where was the woman he fell in love with? "He's not a police officer. I won't answer any questions with him in the room."

"You don't get to dictate who is in the room, Mrs. Berns. Are you going to cooperate or should the officer read you your rights and we'll arrest you?"

She heaved a deep sigh, "Okay," she said quietly.

"Mrs. Berns, did you ever meet Richard Gauvin?"
Susan looked up from her folded hands she was staring at. "I thought this was about the fight at Jus . . . Mr. Wade's condo? Why are you asking me this?"
Lieutenant Chambers glanced at Justin, then back at Susan.

"I'll ask the questions, Mrs. Berns. Your job is to answer them. Again, did you ever meet Richard Gauvin?"

"No, I never met him."

"How about Mrs. Gauvin?"

Susan fidgeted in her chair. "Once, when I went to her travel agency, and I tried to call her about my husband but she wouldn't take my calls."

"What did you go there for, Mrs. Berns?"

"To book a trip."

"To where?"

"I don't know. I went there to decide but left before I decided."

"Why did you leave without deciding?"

"Someone diverted my attention and I left."

"Who was that Mrs. Berns?"

"This man, here,"" she said pointing to Justin.

Lieutenant Chambers gave Justin one of those *what-where-you-up-to* looks.

"What happened Mrs. Berns?"

"He came in behind me. He surprised me. I thought he was someplace else. We were planning on going away together, to live off my dead husband's insurance money."

Lieutenant Chambers turned to Justin. He did not look happy. "Is that true Mr. Wade?"

"Not entirely, Lieutenant. The offer was made . . . it was a tempting offer but I hadn't accepted. I was leaning in the direction of saying no."

"And why would you turn down such a lucrative offer, Mr. Wade?"

What happened to keep my mouth shut? Justin looked at his buddy, John Muldoon.

John nodded.

"As John will tell you, I discussed my reservations with him. Something I couldn't put my finger on, until now. There's an evil side of her, Lieutenant. She . . ."

"Never mind the name calling, Mr. Wade." Lieutenant Chambers said and turned to Susan. "Let's continue, Mrs. Berns."

Susan's eyes blazed hatred across the table at Justin. The atmosphere was charged with animosity.

"Have you ever been to the Gauvin home, Mrs. Berns?"

"No."

"Have you any idea who killed Mr. Gauvin, Mrs. Berns?"

Her eye's darted from Lieutenant Chambers to Justin, before looking down at the table. She raised her head defiantly. "No, I have no idea."

"Some of our investigators think you killed Richard Gauvin, Mrs. Berns. What do you have to say about that?"

She stood up. "That's it! I'm done here. I want a lawyer."

"Suite yourself, Mrs. Berns, we'll book you on suspicion. Once you're through booking, we'll let you make that phone call."

Justin watched as Sergeant Muldoon, took her by the elbow and escorted her out of the room. "I'm sorry, Susan," John said as they walked down the hall.

"Don't feel sorry for me, John. Before this is over I'll have all your badges." She turned and looked at Justin standing outside the interrogation room door. "And him, I'll sue his ass for defamation of character."
John shook his head at Justin. "Book her," he said to the officer behind the desk. "And contact Judge Hayes and request a large bail. She may be a runner."

With Susan being processed, Lieutenant Chambers motioned to John and Justin to come back into the interrogation room.

"As you probably know, the Russian Oleg Popov was beat up outside of the Sea Shell Motel."

"I may have heard something about that," John said.

Chambers looked right at Justin "I don't suppose you have any ideas either, Mr. Wade."

"No sir," Justin said solemnly.

"From this moment on, Wade, you will stay out of this station and away from anyone involved in this investigation. We could face lots of repercussions from the Russian embassy if this guy implicates us in any way. Is that understood?"

"Yes, sir, Lieutenant," Justin said.
On the way out of the station, John whispered to Justin, "Meet me at Bad Boys in twenty minutes."

When Justin entered the restaurant he spotted John sitting at a table with Dorothy. He walked over and sat heavily in the chair.

Dorothy spoke first. "I'm sorry it didn't work out with Susan, Justin. John told me most of it. Wow, talk about an about face."

Justin tried to muster a smile, although it really wasn't in him. "Thanks Dorothy, I guess I'm not as lucky as Ol' Toody here in the women department."

"Slick," John said. "What did you do to that Russian?"

Justin shrugged. "I guess I got carried away. I not only wanted information, but, I guess that I wanted to retaliation for getting knocked on the head. I still have a bump up there. I'm really tired of people trying to beat me up over this damn necklace."

"Speaking of people beating you up," John said. "We let that big guy go. He was an innocent bystander to all of this. He just met Susan last night and she jumped right into bed with him. He thought he was protecting her. Not the brightest star in the galaxy."

Dorothy reached across the table and patted Justin's arm. "I'm sorry about that, Justin. I know you cared for her."

"Yes, I did. But there is something about her that frightens me. I think she may be involved in this mess, in some way. Anyway, John, would you let me know what goes on when her lawyer gets down here. I also want to know if and when she's released. Can you do that?"

"Of course, Slick. Nothing will change between you and I because of Chambers. He's just a politician cop. I really dislike those guys, as you know."

"Thanks, John."

They ordered lunch and chatted as they ate. Justin kissed Dorothy goodbye, shook John's hand and they drove off in different directions.

Chapter Fifteen

Goldfinger. Damn phone. Justin groggily reached for his cell "Yeah?' He looked at the clock beside his bed. Six a.m. "Who the hell is waking me up at this hour?"

"Slick. It's John."

"Toody, sorry to bite your head off. I swear, this is why I turn my cell off. Every morning, without fail, the damn thing wakes me up. What's up?"

"We just received a fax," John said. "It seems that Russian, Oleg Popov, is an ex-K.G.B. operative. How does that grab you?"

"I guess their government is serious about getting the necklace back, huh? Where did that info come from?"

"Direct from the F.B.I., Slick. In fact, the F.B.I. and the C.I.A. will be here in the morning. They want to track down Popov before he leaves the country. They don't want us farmers to create some sort of incident." Justin heard the smile in John's voice. "Chambers can't prove it unless he conducts an official investigation, but he knows you're the one that messed up the guy. Politicians certainly don't rock their own boats over any *incidents.* An investigation by the Feds is not going to help his political career."

"Well, maybe in time he'll get over my messing up Popov a little bit. The guy really pissed me off. Besides, Chambers is the one who set him loose."

"Find the person that killed Gauvin and I'm sure he'll forgive you. He doesn't give a rat's ass about the necklace. That's the job of the police up north. He wants to crack the killing. It's a Naples thing and murders shake up this little town. Not that I blame them . . . nobody wants this place to turn into another Miami."

"Okay, John. I'm going to try to go back to sleep. Give me a ring when Susan's lawyers arrive, okay Pal?"

"Got it."

Justin rolled over and fell back into dreamless sleep.

When he awoke, he was fresh and relaxed. It had been the first time in long while that he'd slept so late, if ten in the morning was considered late.

Eggs were cooking in the frying pan and the coffee pot was perking, sending the aroma of fresh coffee drifting through Justin's apartment. He tilted the frying pan sliding the eggs into a plate as the doorbell rang. Justin grabbed his hospital scrub pants and slipped them on. He opened the door to find Rochelle Gauvin standing in front of him.

"Rochelle! This is a surprise. Come in. How did you find where I live?" Thank God he didn't answer the door in his skivvies.

"Mrs. Berns gave me the address when she was in my agency. You remember that day, don't you? That was the day you came in and whisked her out. Remember?"

"Yes, I remember. What can I do for you, Rochelle?"

"I wanted to tell you that I lied to you. We did have the necklace. We had it hidden in our home. Not very well, apparently. Somebody found it and murdered my husband. Believe me when I tell you; I have no idea who has it. I talked to Richard the night before he was killed. I can't tell you the exact conversation but I think he mentioned the name Berns. He was scheduled to have a meeting with somebody. I didn't understand it all, and at the time, I thought he was talking about Mr. Berns, the man that was killed in Boston. The more I think about that conversation, the more I think he said *Mrs*. Berns, not *Mr*. Berns. She may know something."

"I'll look into it, Rochelle. I appreciate your coming to see me. Have you told the police, yet?"

"No. I'll let you tell them. I don't like the way they treated me. Anything I have to say to them, they'll have to drag out of me. You seem to be an honest person, Justin. I'll only talk with you."

"Thanks," Justin said as he walked her to the door.

Back in the kitchen, Justin stared at the cold eggs. He dumped them into the sink, dressed and drove to the nearby Dunkin donuts for a dozen filled donut holes and coffee. Leaving the donut shop, he drove toward the Naples police station, placing a call to John as he drove.

"Sergeant Muldoon speaking. How may I help you?"

"Toody, it's me. I've got to talk to you about Susan."

"Morning again, Slick," John said. "I was just about to call you. Susan's attorneys is here. They're in with Chambers as we speak."

"I'll wait in the back parking lot of the station. Would you fill me in as soon as you can?"

"Park in the far corner, Justin. Don't let Chambers see you if he leaves the building."

"Okay, Listen. Rochelle Gauvin came to my place this morning. She confessed that she had the necklace, but it was stolen when her husband was killed. She also thinks Susan's involved. Her name was mentioned by her husband the night before his death. I'd like a crack at Susan. She seems to really hate me now. If I piss her off enough, she might talk. "

"Wait for me out back, Justin. I'll be out as soon as I can."

Justin drove to the far corner of the police parking lot and waited for John to exit the station and come toward his car.

John leaned into the open window.

"Susan is being released into the custody of her lawyers. No bail is being set, so she'll be coming out of the station within the hour. What do you intend to do? Oh hell, Justin. Forget I asked. I don't want to know." Justin chuckled as he watched John walk back into the station.

It was an hour and twenty minutes before Susan exited and walked with her lawyers to a black limousine. Justin followed from a distance as they made their way to the Ritz Carlton Hotel. He watched from behind the large glass doors leading to the beach. Both men signed registration cards. Okay, that meant two separate rooms. Susan signed in next. Maybe he could confront her in her room without the lawyers getting to her.

Susan and the older lawyer left the hotel together. Justin raced back to his car and followed the limousine as it wound its way through the busy traffic. It headed down Davis Boulevard, toward his condo. Strange. Why would they be going to his place? How should he handle that? Beat them home and be there when they arrive? No, he could never get ahead of them without causing attention to himself. He allowed them a large leash and they pulled into his parking space at the rear of the building. Justin watched them enter the building before he pulled alongside the waiting stretch limo.

He glanced at the limo driver as he walked into the building. *Looks like an ex-cop.* He took the elevator to his floor, exiting to see Susan and the elderly lawyer standing in front of his door, along with the president of the association, about to unlock his door.

"Hey! Get away from that door!" Justin pushed the association president aside. "What the hell do you think you're doing? You open my door for everybody that asks?"

The balding little weasel shrunk inside his collar. "I thought you'd want me to open it for your lady friend, Mr. Wade."

"I didn't give you permission to let anyone into my condo. This is a blatant disregard for the condo rules. And I believe it could be considered Breaking and Entering. Isn't that so, Mr. Hotshot Lawyer?"

"Mr. Wade," the lawyer said, looking indignant. Justin cut him short, "You'd better watch your mouth old man or I'll have your ass arrested for B and E. You're lucky I caught you before you went inside."

"I want my things," Susan said, stomping her foot.

"So you think you can just break in to get them? Here, take it." He tossed the bag at her.

The daggers that shot from Susan's eyes brought a smile to Justin's face. He *should* have left them in the hallway, but he retrieved them so he didn't create an issue with his neighbors. They were sticklers for following the rules - apparently more so than the manager. Or had he subconsciously wanted to see her again? The classy lady that Susan once portrayed had disappeared. He slammed the door in her face. Justin vowed that if she were involved in any aspect of this case, he would come down on her with both feet. He went into the kitchen to quench his thirst with a cold beer. The doorbell rang. Now what? He opened the door to see Susan's elderly attorney.

"Now what the hell do you want?" Justin asked.

"I need to inform you that Mrs. Berns no longer needs your services. I'll make sure you get paid for the services provided up to this point."

"You're damn right you will. She and I never discussed my rates, but I'd be glad to submit an invoice for the hours of service performed. Where should I send the invoice?"

The man handed him a card with his Boston address on it.

"I expect payment in full upon receipt," Justin said, trying to sound as menacing as possible.

The man nodded without answering.

Justin felt a little sorry for the old man as he walked away. He had his hands full with that dame.

He really wanted to get to Susan alone. A visit was in order, but he would need some help to get into her hotel room. He placed a call to Rochelle and spelled out what he needed her to do. She agreed to meet him at her travel agency that evening.

Rochelle called Susan's hotel room and requested that she talk to her that evening, at her hotel, or at Rochelle's agency. Susan, after first declining her request, gave in, and asked Rochelle to come to the hotel. Justin and Rochelle took the elevator up to Susan's floor. Justin hid around the corner of the hallway as Rochelle went to Susan's door.

Justin left his hiding place and listened at the door. A housekeeper walked down the hall with an armload of towels. He had to walk away so he wouldn't look suspicious, loitering in the hall. He hoped no one was watching on the security cameras at the front desk.

He waited around the corner, hoping Rochelle would linger in the doorway and give him time to get inside before Susan shut the door. The door suddenly opened and he overheard Rochelle, standing in the doorway.

"Okay, I'll go. But now I believe what I've been hearing. It probably was you that killed my husband. If that's what happened, why involve a private detective?"

"Why? To find my husband, of course."

"I'll be leaving now, Mrs. Berns. I expect to see you again . . . in court." She was stalling in the doorway. Good job Rochelle.

Justin slipped past Rochelle and into the room as she quickly left. Susan jumped at his sudden appearance. Good. He hoped he scared her.

"What are you doing here?" she spat.

"We need to have a little conversation, Susan. Don't worry, I'm not going to touch you . . . ever again."

"I'm not going to talk to you. Get the hell out of here!"

Justin closed the door and crossed his arms across this chest. "Not until you answer some questions."

Susan tried to reach for her cell phone but Justin blocked her way and retrieved it off the table. He tucked her phone in his pants pocket.

Panic crossed her face. He couldn't help but think back to the first time he saw her. She looked so beautiful and classy. Now she was hardly recognizable. "You killed Richard Gauvin, didn't you, Susan?"

Her stare bore like venom into him.

"Son-of-a-bitch," Justin whispered. "You did do it. You shot him in the head!"

"What if I did? Do you really think anybody's going to believe that? I'll deny everything. You can't prove anything." She tried to stare him down.

"Why?" Justin asked. "Why did you kill Richard Gauvin?

"Because he wouldn't fork it over."

"So, you have the necklace?"

She smirked at him. "I have no idea what you are talking about."

"Seriously? I see. So, what now, Susan?"
She sneered. "When I get through all this I'll be going away, with somebody else."

"Not surprising, Susan. I suppose you would have dumped me as soon as we got to an island anyway, huh?"

"Of course, you fool. I was really surprised when you said no."
The conversation was so ludicrous it was funny. "It wasn't that hard a choice, Susan. I saw things in you that weren't pretty. You are a true Jekyll and Hyde. But that's all in the past. You're not going to get away with this."

"Of course I will. Do you think these Keystone Kops are going to stop me? You met my lawyers. My lawyers will make minced meat out of these hicks."

"Where's the necklace, Susan?" Justin asked.

"Get the hell out of here before I call security."
She grabbed the doorknob and yanked the door open.

Justin took his time making his way to the door. "Of course, Susan. I'll see you in court."

"You'll never see me again."

Justin laughed, "Oh, yes I will, Susan." He lifted his jacket for Susan to see the recorder that was inside the breast pocket of his jacket. He tossed Susan's cell phone on the sofa and closed the door behind him before she could respond.

Chapter Sixteen

Justin had just settled down with a beer in hand when there was a knock at his door. Justin looked threw the peep hole to see a distorted version of the old attorney of Susan's. He flung open the door.

"What do you want? I'm busy." Justin said.

"Mr. Wade, Mrs. Berns informed me about what you have done, in her hotel room. You do know that's against the law, don't you?"

"What's against the law, mister . . . what's your name?"

"Ralph Davis. Now, where were we?"
Justin crossed his arms across his chest. "I think you were about to ask me for a certain recording. Am I correct, Mr. Davis?"

Davis looked nervous. Beads of sweat formed across his forehead and on his balding head. Something wasn't right. Justin looked passed him and looked both ways down the hall. A big burly man entered the hall from the stairwell. Another of equal size exited the elevator.

Justin pushed the old man to the ground, out of the path of any fire and drew his pistol from the shoulder harness he wore.

One of the men walked toward his apartment, his arm swinging freely, gun in hand.

Justin dove, hitting the floor and rolling against the wall, with his gun drawn.

The second man raised his weapon to fire.

"Police, drop your weapon!"

Justin looked behind him to see John emerging from the opposite stairwell, gun drawn and pointed at the two men.

How did John know to come now? His timing couldn't be more perfect. Justin might have been able to take one out, but the other probably would have nailed him.

The hit men froze for a second. With four guns drawn, two per side, it could go either way. The tallest took aim at Justin and fired.

Justin's reaction was good and he jerked his head to the left as the bullet whizzed by and landed in the wall behind him.

John fired two shots before Justin had a chance to fire even one.

One man was thrown back against the wall. He slid down to the floor, showing large, paint-like brush strokes of bright red blood on the wall behind him. The second gunman was able to make it to the stairwell and tried to scurry away, leaving a trail of blood from the gunshot wound to his leg. John raced behind him down the steps.

Justin breathed a sigh of relief. He hoped John had back-up downstairs that would meet the guy exiting the building.

The old lawyer untangled his arms from around his head where he lay slumped on the floor in the doorway of the condo. A wet spot spread at the crotch of his trousers.

Justin could hear the officers outside from his spot in the hall. "We got him, Muldoon," one said. "He fired at us and missed. He's dead."

"Good job guys." John said. "Call it in, will you. I'll be upstairs." He climbed back up the stairs and offered a Justin a hand up from the floor. "You all right?"

Justin nodded and accepted his hand. "How the hell did you know I need help right at this second? You're awesome, man."

John holstered his weapon, and walked over to the man by the elevator. He placed his two fingers on the neck and shook his head.

"Actually, I was on my way here to talk to you about something else, and I saw these two big goons enter your building. When one took the stairs and the other took the elevator, something told me it wasn't kosher. Hope your home owners insurance covers bullet holes and blood stains.

"Your instincts are spot on. But why the back-up downstairs if it was a casual visit?" Justin asked.

The lawyer tried to slip by them without saying anything.

"Whoa. Just where do you think you're going?" John blocked the little man from entering the hallway. He looked at the stain across the man's trousers. "I don't think you're cut out for the hit man business."

"I . . . I didn't know they were going to shoot anyone. I was only here to talk to Mr. Wade about the tape."

John looked at Justin. "What tape?"

"I was about to call you about that when all this happened."

Mr. Davis straightened his jacket and stood erect, doing his best to look like the powerful Boston lawyer he once was, even with pee stains down his front. Justin guessed that the man was wishing he'd left this job for his younger, more eager colleagues.

"Mr. Wade used false pretentions to enter Mrs. Berns hotel room. Then he proceeded to provoke her into a confession of Richard Gauvin's demise. All of this is totally false and a tape will never stand up in court. His actions are completely unethical and illegal. I am here to claim that tape."

John gave Justin a stern look. "Well, Mr. Davis. As much as Justin may have acted irrationally, I cannot let you have that tape. This is still an open murder investigation. I will have to confiscate it and put it in police evidence. Whether or not it is admissible in court is up to a judge. I'm not going to arrest you at this time, but stay in town. We will want to talk to you more about your connection in all this." John waved his hand toward the body lying in the hallway.

The little man huffed and stomped past them and headed for the elevator without answering. Waiting for the car, he looked at the blood smear on the wall and the body slumped on the floor. He pulled a handkerchief from his breast pocket and covered his mouth and nose.

The elevator door opened with a police forensic team and the coroner. Mr. Davis made his exit. The team started doing their thing while John led Justin to the small table in the kitchen of his condo.

"Okay, talk Justin. What did you do?"

Justin shrugged and set the recorder on the table. "I got a confession out of Susan. She did it. Killed Richard Gauvin and I think she has the necklace."

"Davis is right, you know. That recording is worthless. And since the necklace was rightfully hers in the first place, it doesn't leave us much to go on."

"You've got to bring her back in. She did it, John. She's your murderer."

"Okay, Slick. Let's say I go get her. What do I hold her on? I can't use the tape. In fact, you may have just given her a ticket to get off scot free. You messed up big time Slick."

Justin stared at the recorder on the table. Damn. Sometimes trying to work within the framework of the law sucks.

"What about arresting her for putting a hit out on me? That's as clear as day. Mr. Davis shows up here with two goons who try to blow my brains out."

John nodded. "I can arrest her for suspicion of attempted murder on you. That's true. But with her lawyers around, they'll advise her to clam up. Perhaps since she was already brought in on suspicion of murder of Gauvin, the judge will hold her without bail this time. I doubt any amount of money will hold her."

Justin raced ahead of his friend to the Ritz. He wanted to make sure they didn't leave. Susan and the two attorneys were sitting in the bar. The old man had changed his pants. Justin chuckled to himself. Old Boston lawyer was over his head in little old Naples, Florida. He met John in the lobby.

"Are they here?" John asked.

"Yes. They're sitting at the bar" Justin said, smiling. They walked into the lounge, and stood behind Susan and her attorney.

"Well, Mr. Davis, we meet again. You've had an exciting evening tonight, haven't you?" John said, smiling, looking at the man's trousers instead of his face.

"We're taking you in for attempted murder, Mr. Davis. You also, Susan. You really shouldn't have tried to kill my friend. Who knows, perhaps we'll finally tie you to the Gauvin murder while we are at it."

The young lawyer began to protest. Chest puffed out, "You have no proof that Mrs. Berns or we had anything to do with whatever happened to Mr. Wade."

Mr. Davis turned to Susan. "I was only there to talk to Mr. Wade. I don't know anything about those men."

"Come on. Let's go. All of you are being held under suspicion." John looked directly at the young lawyer. Maybe he wasn't involved, but John didn't like his Boston better-than-you attitude.

"Very well," Mr. Davis said. "The sooner we clear ours and Mrs. Berns name from all this the better. Then we'll see about suing YOU for defamation of character."

Justin followed John to the station house and against Lieutenant Chambers' orders, he was allowed to watch the interrogation from the two-way glass in the next room.

John brought Mr. Davis in first.

"Okay, Mr. Davis," John said. "Tell me what took place tonight."

"Mrs. Berns informed me that Justin Wade had provoked a false confession out of her in her hotel room and made a tape of it. I was going to retrieve that tape when those two men started shooting at Mr. Wade. Then you showed up and killed one of them. That is all I know."

"And you knew nothing about those men? Weren't they, in fact, hired by Susan Berns to shut Justin up? Perhaps you hired those guys on her behalf."

"Of course not. I had never seen those men before tonight."

"You realize, Mr. Davis, that the only persons that knew of the tape were Susan and Mr. Wade. That certainly would point to Susan ordering a hit on Justin."

"I've already told you. I have no knowledge of any hit ordered by Mrs. Berns."

"Have you been Mrs. Berns family council for a long time, Mr. Davis?

"For about ten years. I met Mr. Berns at the Brookline Tennis Club, where I used to be quite active. Mr. Berns hired me to handle some personal matters and we have been good friends ever since."

"Was Mr. Berns an honest person . . . as far as you know?"

"As far as I knew, yes, he was."

"I'm sure you want to find out who murdered him as much as we do. Was he a gambler, Mr. Davis?"

John's good, thought Justin, watching behind the glass. He's taking him into a comfort zone, out of the line of fire, so he'll open up.

"I'm afraid so," said Davis, nodding. "That's common knowledge. I'm not divulging any family secrets there."

"That is all for now, Mr. Davis. I think it is time to talk to Susan."

"I have advised her not to speak without the presence of an attorney."

"Very well, let's see what she has to say."
John left the room to bring in Susan.

Davis looked nervous, continually wiping his
brow and bald head with his handkerchief. He'd break
easily. This was not the type of cases he was used to
doing in Boston. His specialty was family trust and
insurance litigation.

Sergeant John Muldoon brought Susan in and sat
her at the long metal table facing the glass wall where
Justin watching behind it and could see her face.

"Susan . . . What's happened to you? I'm sincerely
troubled over all of this. I know that Justin thought he
finally found the woman he was looking for. He was in
love with you, you know."

"So, men fall in love with me all the time. I might
have fallen in love with him too, but he spoiled
everything by turning into a jerk."

Mr. Davis walked over to her and talked softly
into her ear, but not so low that John and Justin could not
hear. "You don't have to say a word here, Susan."

She brushed him aside with a wave of her hand.

John shook his head. "Well, I'm sorry to hear that.
I guess we should get down to business."

Justin wanted to come through the glass. *What?*
John was going to let her get away with calling him a
jerk? *I was the jerk? Seriously?*

John continued without responding to the jerk
comment. "Susan, you sent those two guys after Justin,
didn't you?"

"Don't answer them, Susan." Said Davis.

"I don't know anything about two guys going after
Justin. He seems to make enemies pretty easy."

"Susan. You sent two guys to kill Justin if your attorney didn't get the tape back. In fact, by the timing, I'm not sure you really cared it if Justin handed it over. Those guys weren't waiting around for any answers"

"I did nothing of the sort. Why would I put myself in the middle of a murder since that tape is inadmissible and doesn't exist according to the la . . "

She looked at Mr. Davis for confirmation. He nodded, stared at her for a moment, and then spoke.

"Susan, you do realize that you are implicating me in all of this. I had no idea those men were behind me with intention to kill Mr. Wade. I'm not willing to go to prison for you. I've always worked to make things easier for you and Sterling. Why would you do this?"

"I didn't do anything, Ralph. I didn't set you up."

"No? But you hired a hit on Mr. Wade. Why? The tape is meaningless."

Susan was silent. John, listening to their conversation asked, "Mr. Davis, were you at Mr. Berns' wake?"

Davis looked up in surprise. "Of course. What does that have to do with any of this?"

"Just answer the question, Mr. Davis. Did you attend Mr. Bern's wake? Was it an open casket?" John asked.

"No. Susan requested that the casket be closed."

"Thank you, Mr. Davis. At this time, we are not placing you under arrest unless Mr. Wade wants to press charges against you, however, as for your client . . ." John turned to Susan. "Susan Berns, you are under arrest for the murder of Richard Gauvin and the attempted murder of Justin Wade." John went to the door and summoned a uniformed officer. "Read her rights."

John met Justin in the hall and they walked together to John's office.

"We need to contact the Brookline, Massachusetts police. Call it a hunch, but I believe Mr. Berns is alive and they should consider having the body they buried exhumed."

Susan Berns was led away, handcuffed behind her back to the processing room. Justin's eyes met hers for a moment before Justin looked away. How could he have been so wrong about someone? Would he ever learn to trust another woman? His faith was shattered.

"Come on, Slick," John said, as he put his arm around his shoulder. "Let's get some coffee . . . then we have work to do." They walked silently out of the station.

Chapter Seventeen

Boris and Helga left T.G.I. Fridays, and drove down Fifth Avenue to the beach, where they parked and sat in the sand. They stared at the ocean.

"What now, Boris?"

"I don't know, Helga. I'd like to get Oleg and leave, but I can't. I promised Comrade Kazinsky that we would accomplish this mission for him."

Helga turned and faced him, her hair blowing softly in her face. "Comrade Kazinsky?"

"Yes, it was he that sent us. The necklace we are looking for belongs to the Kremlin. It was a gift to the wife of the Czar before the revolution. Its value is fifteen million American dollars."

Her mouth formed in a perfect oval. "Fifteen million?" Helga asked.

Boris nodded. "Yes. Oleg and I were to get five million each, if we were successful in the recovery."

"Oh, my, and my participation? Was that worth anything?"

"Believe me, Helga. I planned to give you a half million. But after our reunion, I've changed my mind."

She pulled away and turned her back toward him. "Don't you think I was worth a half million for doing what I did for you?"

Boris smiled and pulled her close to him.

"My beautiful Helga. I changed my mind because I want to go away with you. I want to take that five million and share it *all* with you. But that all happens *only* if we get the necklace."

"We have to get that necklace, Boris. I want to spend the rest of my life with you."

Boris leaned over and kissed her on the cheek. "We'll get it, Helga." He rose and helped her to her feet.

When they arrived at the Holiday Inn, Boris handed her the key.

"You go ahead, Helga. I'm going to find a newspaper."

He walked away when he heard a ruckus coming from their room. He pulled his gun from his leg harness under his pant leg and crept up to the side of the open door.

"Ivan, what are you doing here?" Boris heard Helga say, alarm in her voice.

"I came to take you home. You're here with Mr. Valentine? You think I don't remember that was Boris Lushin's code name? Is that who you are here with?"

Boris froze. Should he burst through the door, bullets flying or should he wait to see if Helga could handle it? *Wait,* he told himself. Don't do anything that could harm Helga.

"Ivan . . . please, it's not as it looks." Helga sounded frightened. "I'm here on a job. I'm helping him locate something for Comrade Kazinsky. He sent Boris here . . . with Oleg Popov."

"Is that why your clothes are hanging in the closet, Helga, with *his* clothes? And your cosmetics are in *his* bathroom? Don't lie to me, Helga. I am not stupid. You forget, we worked at the same place. If you leave with me now I'll forgive this indiscretion. Come home with me. I want you back. We should never have been divorced. I still love you Helga."

Time to intercede. There was no way Boris was going to let Ivan take Helga back to Boston.

Boris walked through the open doorway, reading the newspaper, trying to look nonchalant, his pistol hidden in the folds of the paper.

"Boris . . . Ivan is here." Helga said nervously.

Boris looked up to see the pistol aimed at him. "Ivan, nice seeing you again, but that is hardly necessary. What is the point of this? Please put it away."

"No, Boris. You should know better. I can never stand for this. You knew what sort of man I was. I am still that man, Boris."

Boris took note of the silencer on the automatic pistol pointed at him.

"Ivan, please. Don't do anything stupid. Nothing has happened between us. We are only working together."

"I don't believe you. Sit down Boris."

Boris folding his gun in the newspaper and sat it beside the arm chair by the bed.

"Sit," Ivan ordered. He pulled the cord from a table lamp and tore it from its base. He threw it to Helga.

"Tie his hands behind his back, Helga. And don't make me shoot you. Tie him tight."

Boris could see Helga trembling. "Do as he says, Helga. Don't put your own life in danger.

She did what Ivan ordered. "Ivan, please don't do this! I'll come home with you, right now."

"Yes, you will. Pack your things quickly." Ivan kept his eye on both of them as she packed. "Wait for me in the lobby, Helga." He waved the gun toward the door.

Tears coursed down her cheeks. "No, Ivan. Please, don't do this."

"Go," he shouted. "I need to talk to your friend."

Ivan walked to the side of Boris. If only he would cross in front of him, then Boris would have a chance to kick his feet out from under him.

"Boris, I worked for you for a long time. Did you think we were friends? We weren't. I've always disliked you. You're always so smug, you think you're better than everybody else. Even your partner, Oleg dislikes you. Did you know that? He only works with you because your team received more benefits than all the others. So, my friend. Our talk is over. You will not bother me or Helga again." Ivan pointed his gun at Boris' forehead.

Boris had to think fast. "Ivan, don't do this. I will never . . ." . . .

Those were his last words. A dull thud from the silencer said it all. Brains spattered against the ugly green plaid curtains.

Ivan walked from the room, placing a do not disturb sign on the outside door knob. He picked up Helga's luggage and threw them into the trunk of the rental car. Neither spoke as they drove away. Helga cried softly into her hands.

"Stop, Helga. You are my wife, you shouldn't have run off as you did. And to make it worse, you slept with him."

"Did you kill him?" She asked.

"Of course not. We just talked"

She stared at Ivan. "Really? You didn't shoot him?"

"No. But he won't bother us again. I convinced him that he should stay away." Helga didn't answer him. She wiped her eyes, knowing deep in her heart that she would never see Boris again. Ivan drove to the Naples airport and bought a ticket to the first available flight to Fort Myers. He wanted to get out of Naples as quickly as he could. He planned to catch another flight to Europe from what-ever city he landed in.

Chapter Eighteen

Justin tried to pack up the boxes at his old office which he was moving into the new space. He was going to start over and get a fresh start in a nice clean new office. His phone rattled under a stack of old newspapers he was using for packing material. He dug under the papers to grab it before it went to voice mail. He hit the speaker to listen to the message.

"Damn it Justin!" John said. "Will you please keep your cell phone on? I've been calling all over town, looking for you."

"I hate that damn thing. No privacy. What's up?"

"Look, meet me right away at the Holiday Inn. I have a surprise for you."

"What is it, John? I don't have time for surprises."

"We found the second Russian. He was shot through the head."

"Are you there, now?" Justin asked.

"Yes"

Justin dropped the autographed copy of Luis Tiant (1971-1978), about the famous Boston Red Sox pitcher. "I'm on my way."

Justin arrived at the same time that Sandy, the female undercover police officer arrived. They walked into the lobby together. John was standing outside the room where Boris' body was found.

"Good, you're both here. We can't go into the room yet, forensic is inside doing their thing. Sandy, I need you to identify this guy. You and Justin are the only people that came face to face with him, if this *is* him."

John told a uniformed officer to let them know when they could enter the room.

"Sandy, Justin, let's go grab some lunch while we wait. I'm buying. Might not have much of an appetite after you go in there."

Two hours later the uniformed officer came to their table and told them the room is clear. They walked into the room, where a blood soaked sheet covered Boris' head and body.

John lifted the sheet as Sandy and Justin viewed the body.

"That's him," Sandy said, turning away as her face paled. There wasn't a lot left of his face to recognize.

Justin nodded. "Yes. That's him."

"A bullet through the head." Justin said. "That's the second one in a week. Susan's in jail, so unless she was able to order a hit from inside, she couldn't be responsible for this one. I think we have a second shooter here in Naples, John. Somebody we haven't thought of. Have you heard anything new from the Boston police?"

"They agreed to exhume the body of Sterling Berns. I expect something any time now. Let's get back to the station."

"What about Lieutenant Chambers?"

"Screw him!" John snapped.

A fax was waiting for John when he arrived at the police station.

"So, this is Sterling Berns," Justin said, with a smile. "He looks a bit older than Susan, wouldn't you say, John?"

"Yeah, he is. Did I forget to mention that to you? He is almost twenty years Susan's senior."

"She probably married him for his money," Justin said, sarcastically.

"Well, as long as she made him happy."

"I suppose you're right, Toody," Justin said, shrugging his shoulders. "So, what do we do now? How are we going to find this other guy?"

"It's all still tied to Susan somehow." John said.

"Can I try talking to her again, John?"

"I don't have any other leads, so why not? Maybe you can get something new out of her."

Justin walked into the cell area along with John.

"Susan," John said. I think you'd better listen to what Justin has to say. I'll be outside." Justin was let into Susan's cell. He leaned against the grey concrete wall.

"Susan, you're in a lot of trouble. They found the body of one of those Russians. He was shot in the head, the same as Richard Gauvin. They're going to charge you with at least one of the murders, and also fraud. The fraud is the lesser of the charges, Susan. You filed an insurance claim and you have the necklace. The Lieutenant's going to ask the DA to go for the death penalty."

"I didn't kill Richard Gauvin!"

"But you killed the Russian?"

"No."

"You already confessed to killing Gauvin, to me . . . remember?" Justin said.

Susan never looked so bad. Not just the orange scrubs, but with no make-up, she had dark circles under her eyes. She had the look of a beaten woman.

"I don't want to go to prison, Justin. I'd never survive. What should I do?"

"Let's start with the truth. I suggest you make a statement. I'll get John in here. I agree with you, Susan. You'd never survive in prison."

"I'll make a statement. I'll tell John what he wants to know. But only if we can make a deal. No prison time."

Justin left the cell and returned after a few minutes with John. Along with a uniformed officer, a tape recorder and a stenographer, they moved Susan to an interrogation room.

"Susan, this is how this is going to happen. I will listen to your statement, then I will decide if I can offer any type of deal."

"If I'm innocent of any crime, will you deal with me?" she asked. She looked genuinely afraid.

"If you're innocent, I'll do everything I can do. If you cooperate, I'll help." John nodded to the stenographer to turn on the recorder.

"What is your name?"

"Susan Berns."

"Do you request your attorney to be present?"

"No, that is not necessary."

"What is your husband's name?"

"Sterling Berns."

"Is what you are about to tell us of your own free will?"

"Yes, it is."

"What is your home address?"

"222 Commonwealth Avenue, Boston, Massachusetts"

"Do you live there with your husband?"

"Yes."

"Is your husband dead?"

"No . . . he isn't"

What? Justin looked at John. What the hell is going on?

"Your husband, Sterling Berns is alive?" asked John.

"Yes."

"Who was buried in his place?"

Susan looked down at her hands, picking at her chipped nail polish. "Some man that resembled Sterling."

"You were aware that Sterling Berns was alive when you filed for his life insurance?"

"Of course, yes." Her voice got softer with each revelation.

"Where is Sterling Berns, right now?"

"He has a room at the Wellesley Inn, here in Naples." Her voice was barely above a whisper.

John fiddled with the volume on the recorder. "Speak up so the recorder can catch your voice, Susan. Who killed Richard Gauvin?"

"Sterling did."

Damn. Their supposedly dead victim was alive AND the murderer of Richard Gauvin.

John continued. "Why did you confess to Justin Wade that you killed Richard Gauvin?"

She turned in her chair and met Justin's cold stare.

"I wanted to throw him off track."

"Why?"

"To protect Sterling. I didn't want anyone to know he was alive and had killed Gauvin."

"Is your husband registered at the Wellesley Inn?"

"Yes."

"Under what name?"

"I believe John Smith."

John stopped the tape recorder and whispered in the ear of the uniformed officer. *"Pick up Sterling Berns . . . or John Smith, at the Wellesley Inn. Take back up with you."* He re-started the tape recorder. "Did Sterling Berns kill the Russian at the Holiday Inn?"

"I have no idea. I didn't know anyone else was killed."

John tapped on the metal desk with his fingers and glanced back at Justin. "Where is the necklace, Susan . . . the necklace called The Romanov Star?"

"It's in Boston . . . in our safe deposit box."

"Tell us, in order of events what took place from the start."

Susan sighed. "Where do I start?"

"I suggest at the beginning, Susan."

"Sterling had large gambling debts. He didn't have the money to pay them off, so he decided to sell the necklace. When Sterling found out that the necklace was worth much more than we initially thought, he increased the insurance on it and found a man that would fence it for him. That was Ken Bucci, from Revere. We found this man, Howard Simon, who looked remarkably like Sterling and had him deliver the necklace. Sterling gave the man his identification, to make it look like it was him. Bucci said that the man opened the package that he was supposed to deliver to Bucci and realized it was worth a lot more than what he was getting. He tried to cut Bucci out, so Bucci killed him. He didn't know it wasn't Sterling. Then he sent the necklace down to the Gauvins, as he was supposed to do."

John interrupted Susan. "And how did you get this information?"

"From Bucci himself. Het threatened to kill me too if I didn't up his share of the split."

"What was the split supposed to be?"

"Bucci was to get one million, we were to get six and the Gauvins' were to get three. But now Bucci wanted three million."

"I take it the real Sterling didn't go for that idea," Justin said.

Susan shook her head. "No. He came here to get the necklace back from Gauvins. He decided he didn't want to split any of the money. He didn't want to sell to those people. He thought he could find his own buyer and keep all the money for himself."

"And you, Susan. You were innocent all this time?" John asked.

"Yes," she answered.

Justin was adding the splits in his head. "That only comes to ten million. I thought the street value was fifteen mil?"

"I don't know about that. All I know is that we were to get ten. Perhaps he thought he could get fifteen from a different buyer, but ten million is a lot of money. We could pay off his gambling debts and still have plenty to live happily on the rest of our lives. I was doing what my husband asked me do. I love my husband and I didn't want our being broke to come between us. If we didn't have money to pay his debts, those gambling sharks probably would have killed him. Everybody got greedy. Gauvin wanted more money too. Sterling couldn't let that happen. He only wanted the necklace back, so he could sell it himself. The day Mrs. Gauvin went out of town Sterling went to the Gauvin home."

"And that is when Sterling killed Gauvin?" John asked.

Susan nodded.

"How did the necklace get up to Boston?" John asked.

"I took it with me when I went for his . . . for Simon's funeral."

"That was the time Justin went up to Boston to see you, and Mr. Bucci?"

"Yes, that's right."

Son-of-a-bitch, Justin mumbled to himself. *She had it all the time.* John shot a look at Justin, telling him to be quiet.

"Why did Sterling stay in Naples?"

"He was hiding out from the bookies. He had to make another sale connection before he could pay them off."

"Did he know the two Russians were here looking for the necklace?"

"Yes. I told him."

"Why are you accusing your husband, Susan?" She ripped a hang nail from the cuticle of her finger. "I don't want to go to prison."

"And what if Sterling goes to prison?"

"Well, he's the one that did the killing. Why should I go to prison for what he did?"

Justin let out a grunt in response. So much for her undying love for he husband. She'd sell him down the river in a second to save her own skin. John shook his head.

"Who was going to give you your share for the necklace, the ten million dollars?"

"Some business man here in Naples. Only my husband knows his name. All I know is he's supposed to be very wealthy builder and respected here in Naples."

"You don't know his name?"

"No."

"Okay, Susan. That's all for now. For the record, tell your name again, and where you live."

"My name is Susan Berns. I live at 222 Commonwealth Avenue, Boston, Massachusetts."

"And the statement you just made was given without any coercion, by anybody?"

"Yes, no coercion. It was given with a promise of no prison time."

John shook his head. "I told you, Susan, no promises. We will weigh all that you've said and somebody above me will make a determination. But rest assured, I will do what I can, seeing that you cooperated."

"Yes sir, Sergeant Muldoon. I understand," Susan said sadly.

Susan was led back to her cell. John and Justin stayed behind to discuss what had transpired.

"What do you think, Justin?" John asked.

"It's your call, John. Do whatever you have to do. What about the other Russian around here someplace? What are the FBI and CIA going to have to say about him?"

"I think that's their problem to find him. I don't think he'll make any more attempts at getting the necklace with his partner dead. The most we could get on him is assault and battery. That's more trouble than it's worth."

"I guess you're right. I've already paid him back for the knock on the head," Justin said, feeling for the bump on his head.

The uniformed officer which was sent to pick up Mr. Berns returned empty handed. "No luck, Sarge. The desk clerk said he hadn't slept in his bed for two nights. The maid reported back to him when she did the room service. Any ideas where we might look?"

"I haven't the slightest idea," John replied. "There's a picture of him on my desk. Have copies made and make sure every officer has a copy. And while you're at it . . . get them over to County. Put an APB out on him. Maybe one of their deputies might spot him. While you're at it, get them to Lieutenant Wells over at Highway Patrol. Tell him this is priority."

"Well, Justin. Not much to do now but wait until we nab him."

Chapter Nineteen

Justin, driving down Airport Road, made a last second decision, hit the brake and swerved into the road that lead into the airport. A last second thought that he might as well check the small airport, caused his car to miss an airport sign by inches. He entered the small terminal and walked to the ticket counter.

"Excuse me, Miss. I'm sure you've been asked by the police about this picture, but I thought I'd check in anyway." He handed the hostess a picture of Sterling Berns.

"Have you seen this guy?"

She was young, with ripped jeans at the knees and a Bon Jovi T-shirt that strained against her small nipples, which were obviously not encased in any bra. She pulled on a string of gum in her mouth. "Yea, cool looking guy, very I-got-the-power look."

Seriously? It was only a hunch. Justin stuttered as he asked, "Do you . . . have you any idea where he was heading?"

"I think so," she said with a snap of her gum. "Key West - think the dude is gay?"

"Key West, huh? When?"

"Last night, the flight log says 7:15 p.m."

If she wasn't under age, he would have kissed her right on the lips. "Do you have any flights leaving for Key West soon?"

She ran her black painted fingernails over the keys of the computer. "Yea, there's a flight leaving in one hour and there are a few open seats."

"Super. Book me and I'll be back before then." He dropped his credit card on the table. "Name's Wade, Justin Wade."

A smile crossed her florescent orange lips "Is that like Bond, James Bond?"

"Absolutely," Justin laughed as he turned and raced out. He returned with five minutes to spare, checked in and boarded the plane. Two men boarded the small plane right after Justin, minutes before they pulled the door shut. Justin glanced up from the newspaper in his lap. One sat in front of him and the other moved down the aisle to a rear seat. Two hours later the small plane touched down in Key West. Justin checked in to a small B&B close to Smathers Beach.

After leaving his bags in his room, Justin grabbed a cab to Duval Street and stopped at Sloppy Joes, the first bar he saw. He showed Sterling Berns picture to the barkeeper. No luck, he didn't recognize him. He continued doing the Duval crawl, a little less fun when totally sober, asking all the barkeepers and servers if they recognized Berns.

The sidewalk sent heat waves from the pavement and even the six-toed ancestors of Hemingway's cats and the chickens seem to be avoiding the hot concrete. Justin stopped and wiped his brow with the sleeve of his shirt. On the corner of Duval and Applerouth, an establishment that looked more upscale than the rest of the store fronts of Duval Street enticed him in for a cool drink.

"Welcome to Virgilio's," an attractive hostess in a skin tight black sheath that left little to the imagination said.

"Thank you. May I sit at the bar?"

"Of course," she said. "I can highly recommend our Scotch. We have the finest on the island." She turned and greeted the couple that arrived behind him.

Nice Ass. Keep in check, Wade. You're here to find a murderer, not hook up. He forced his eyes away from her rear and made his way to the bar.

"Scotch please," he said to the server, dressed well in a white dress shirt and tuxedo pants. Pretty fancy for Key West.

"Would Lagavulin do, sixteen or twenty-one year sir?"

Justin didn't know the difference and he was sure he never had a Scotch by that name. He was a Dewar's guy. About as steep as he went when buying a bottle. What the hell? He could afford one drink. How much could it be? "Twenty one, please."

The bartender raised an eyebrow and gave an appreciative nod. "Yes, sir. Very good choice."

The Scotch was so smooth, Justin had to force himself not to drink it too fast. So this was how the other half lived. He probably could have been drinking Lagavulin twenty-one for the rest of his life if he would have gone along with Susan. No, she wasn't worth it.

He casually looked around the room and did a double take. There in the corner was Sterling Berns. Justin could hardly believe his luck. He checked the picture a number of times before he was convinced it was him. He couldn't confront him in the restaurant. This wasn't the type of place to appreciate a bar-room brawl. So he kept an eye on Berns, while he sipped on the best Scotch he ever tasted in is life, and would probably ever taste again.

An hour passed. How long would it take for Berns to make a move? Justin's glass was empty but he shook his head at the bartender when he wanted to refill his glass. Another thirty minutes passed before Berns rose from his seat, handed the server some bills and walked from the bar. The sun was almost down and shadows were forming up and down the street. Justin looked at his tab and almost choked. He could have really tied one on for that price. He signed his credit card receipt, thankful it didn't get rejected, and followed Berns at a comfortable distance.

Berns walked a few blocks, turned on Olivia, then again on Whitehead Street. Justin noticed a square salt-box home with yellow shutters. The grounds were immaculate and a sign on the corner read, *Ernest Hemingway Home and Museum.* Hmm, if he had the time, he'd like to check that out. Not that Justin was much of a reader, and other than reading *The Sun Also Rises,* required reading in high school, he was sure he'd never read any other books of Hemmingway. Maybe it was the high-class Scotch, giving him a sense of euphoria and sophistication.

Another sense, one of being followed, made Justin turn and see the two men from the airplane behind him about a block. They were talking to each other. Must be coincidence. It was a small island. Berns crossed the street, but Justin stayed on the east side. The two men also crossed the street and picked up their pace. Before he could react, Justin heard a shot, followed by another two shots. Berns staggered and fell.

Justin drew his automatic from under his jacket and returned fire on the two men, firing until the gun was emptied of the five bullets it carried. One man fell. Justin ducked behind a parked car, reloaded a second set of rounds and fired again at the second man. He saw the man fall, holding his arm.

He rushed quickly to the man's side, kicking his gun into the gutter. He grabbed the man by the back of his shirt and dragged him over to the body of Sterling Berns. Justin reached down to feel for a pulse. Nothing. He gripped the man around the wound on his bleeding arm.

"Ahh, that hurts."

"That's the least of you troubles. What's your name?"

The guy didn't answer so Justin squeezed a little harder on the open wound.

"Ahh, ahhh, okay, okay. My name is Carl Kegg.

"Well, Kegg, you're coming with me, you bastard."

Sirens coming closer told Justin that a neighbor must have called the police. He should stay and meet them. And there was Berns' body, and the other guy lying dead on the sidewalk. No, he didn't have the time nor the inclination to get mixed up with the Key West finest. He'd take this guy back to Naples. Then John could call the Key West police and explain. How was he going to pull it off, get the man back to Naples? He dragged the man into the backyard of one of the Florida bungalows. A small bench sat beside a colorful flower garden. Justin shoved the man down onto a bench. He shoved his gun in his jacket pocket, pointing it at the man.

"Who sent you to take out Berns?" Justin said. The man laughed. Justin pushed the barrel of his gun into the man's side.

"Listen, you piece of shit. I don't mind shooting you, and I don't have time to deal with the cops right now, so start talking, NOW."

"Okay, okay," the man said. "If you don't kill me, those Israeli's will when I don't bring them that necklace. I'll talk if you promise me protection."

"I'm not a cop. I can't give you protection."

"I know. We've been following you since Naples. But you have a close cop friend."

Justin shook his head. "Still can't help you, but I can talk to my friend, tell him you cooperated. That's all I can do."

Kegg winced as Justin put more pressure on his wound. Blood dripped down his arm and stained the sun-bleached bench. "That's all that I ask, and a trip to the ER. I'm bleeding to death here."

Justin tore the cloth away from his wound and examined it."

"You'll live. The bullet didn't even lodge. Went right through your fleshy part and out the other side." He tore a piece of Kegg's shirt and tied it around his arm. He pulled it tight and knotted it. "What's this about some Israelis?"

"Two brothers, big contractor in Naples."

"The guys that built Diamond Lakes Golf Community?" Justin asked.

"Yes, that's them."

"Is their name Duke?"

"Yes, it used to be Dukofsky, I was told. I guess they changed it."

"They put the hit on Berns?"

The man nodded, wincing when Justin squeezed his wound a little tighter. "Yes, yes."

"Why?"

"They found out Berns was going to double cross them - keep the necklace, or sell it to a higher bidder."

"And you two guys were ordered to snuff him and bring them the necklace?"

"Yes."

Damn, damn, damn. Justin didn't think to check Berns for the necklace. He wouldn't be carrying around a fifteen million dollar necklace in his pocket, would he?

"You just going to leave my partner and Berns laying in the street?" Kegg asked.

"The Key West police will take care of them, but the necklace. Did you think he had it on him?" Justin said. They'd have to go back, get involved, if the KW police found that necklace.

Kegg shook his head. "Naw, I wasn't supposed to kill him, yet. Just wound him so he could talk. The Duke's think it is here on the island somewhere." He shrugged. I guess I am a better shot than I thought."

"Okay, we're going back to Naples."

"How? Are we gonna get there, drive?"

"No, pal. We're flying, just like we came."
Justin walked him back to his hotel, picked up his bags and they caught a taxi back to the airport. There were no more commercial flights for the night, but there was a pilot that would fly him back for two hundred and fifty dollars. The pilot raised his eyebrows at the sight of Justin and his prey, hands tie-wrapped behind his back, but said nothing. In route to Naples, Justin asked the pilot to have the Naples police meet them at the airport.

As they taxied to the terminal, Justin saw John and a police cruiser waiting outside the terminal, by the gate.

He exited the plane behind his prisoner. Justin held him by his bound arms as they walked to the waiting police.

"Hi, John. Meet Carl Kegg, the *real* Berns killer."

"Damn! Now how are we going to find out who was behind all of this?"

"Not to worry my friend. Kegg here has all the answers." Justin handed off Kegg to a uniformed officer who led him away.

"Kegg had a second hit man with him. Unfortunately I killed him. I left him in the street with Sterling Berns. You better get to the Key West police and smooth things over. I left a mess on the street with two bodies. I hope to God that Berns wasn't carrying around that necklace in his pocket"

John rolled his eyes at him. "You didn't check, AND you left the scene of a crime? For crying out loud, Justin, Are you crazy?"

"I know, probably not the smartest thing I ever did. But I didn't want them to tie me and this guy up. I didn't want to give the money man time to get away."

"Okay," John said. "Who was the money man?"

"Money men," Justin corrected. "The Duke Brothers. The guys that made a mess at the Diamond Lakes project on Davis Boulevard and another project on County Barn Road. You know of them?"

John shook his head. "I don't follow the real estate market down here, but their names sound familiar."

"Well, if Kegg makes a phone call, to collect his money and deliver the necklace . . . ," Justin said.

John ran his fingers through his hair. "They thought Berns still has the necklace? Let me get this straight. They were going to snuff Berns and steal the necklace. Correct?"

"Sounds like it. They heard that Berns changed his mind . . . that he was going to keep the necklace or sell it to a higher bidder. Kegg is willing to give up the Dukes, if he can get some protection. I told him no promise. But, if we use him as the decoy, maybe we can nab them. What do you think?"

"Sounds good to me. Let's get him to the station. I want to include the Lieutenant in on this. I want him to know that it was you that cracked this thing."

"He might not be so pleased when he knows I left the scene of a crime, with the suspect," Justin said, smiling.

"Yea, he's going to blow a gasket and take some heat for that. We'll have to notify the Key West police. But if we solve the murder of Richard Gauvin, he'll kiss and make-up."

"Sounds good to me, Toody," Justin said as he threw his arm around his friend's shoulder.

Lieutenant Chambers was waiting for them as they entered the station. Sergeant Muldoon filled him in and asked him to do the smoothing over in behalf of Justin to the Key West police. Justin and John waited as the Lieutenant agreed and made the phone call.

Justin watched nervously as Chambers came out of his office. He was smiling. Whew! That could have gone very badly.

"That wasn't easy," the Lieutenant said, as he exited his office. "Good thing the Chief in Key West owed me a favor. They were scouring the island for the shooter, closing off A1A and holding air flights. It is a huge mess. I told them to call off the dogs— that his "killer" was in our hands." He looked at Justin, eyes narrowed into slits. "BOTH of them. You killed someone on their turf, even if it was in self-defense." Lieutenant Chambers turned his focus to John. "But, it's all taken care of. Let's make that phone call to the Dukes."

Kegg punched in the numbers of the Duke Brothers from his cell phone. Justin noticed his hand was trembling and sweat dripped from his forehead. His nervousness could blow the whole thing.

"Hello," Kegg said. "I want to talk to Yale Duke. Yes, he's expecting my call. This is Kegg, one of his men in Naples. Tell him it's important. Okay, I'll wait." *(pause)* "Yes, it's done. I've got the necklace and Berns is dead. But so is my partner. The P.I. that we tailed to find Berns shot both of us. I took a hit in the arm, and I need to lay low someplace, out of the area. Where can we make the exchange?" *(pause)* "Yes, I can meet you there. What time? Okay, two hours." He repeated the time for the benefit of those listening in the room. "Okay, the entrance of the Naples pier in two hours."

He looked at Lieutenant Chambers. "Did I do okay? You're going to cover me, right? When he finds out I don't have the necklace, I'm as good as dead."

"We'll have you well covered. Just play it cool," John said.

"You'll speak to the DA in Key West, right? I cooperated so we can plea bargain, right?"

Chambers nodded. "I'll do what I can. Once we nab the Dukes, you'll be heading back to Key West for arraignment." He motioned for his uniformed officer to take him away.

"Lock him up and get him a doctor. Okay, guys," he said, as he turned to John and the other officers in the room. "We have an hour and a half. We'll set a trap for Duke. Let's hope it is only one of them."

He looked at Justin and frowned. "Maybe we could stake out Wade and Sandy on the beach, undercover as lovers. They can cover the sand area and watch for any getaway boats. Wade, don't use a gun unless you use it in self-defense, you got that? One shooting by you is enough. The rest of us will be in plain clothes acting like tourists. Everyone needs to be in place by two a.m. I expect he won't be there alone. He'll probably stay in the car while somebody else does the dirty work. I want the end of the street covered in case they make a run for it. I want people behind the walls of the private property that line the street. Make sure the streets and the beach in the area is clear of tourists and civilians. And most of all, I don't want Kegg harmed in any way. I want to turn him over in good shape. Everybody got all that? Okay, John, ride herd on this. Make sure everything is set up."

John nodded in assent. He turned to Justin. "Have you met Sandy yet? I think by acting like lovers, as the Lieutenant wants, you may have to make it look real on the beach. Are you up to that?"

"Why?" Justin replied. He had met Sandy at the Gauvin house. She was impressive, kept her cool, even when she was tied up by the Russians.

"She kind of cute, in an innocent looking way." A little young for his taste. Then why was Susan's face the only one he could imagine kissing? Damn her for still being in his head. "Can I be the one to tell Susan about her husband, John?"

"Sure," John answered. "I don't think the Lieutenant would mind. But why? Don't tell me you still have feeling for her."

Did he? Justin walked into the cell area. He stood outside the bars as Susan walked toward him.

"Did you find Sterling?" she asked, her hands gripping the bars. She looked vulnerable now, soft and defenseless, not at all like the cold-hearted woman that let greed ruin her.

"Yes. Susan, he was in Key West."

Her knuckles turned white from gripping the bars. "Was? . . . What are you saying?"

"He was shot . . . he's dead, Susan. The buyer for the necklace put a hit out on him. He thought Sterling was double-crossing him. We hope to pick him up in a few hours."

Susan's entire body appeared to shrink. She moved to the simple grey cot and sat on the edge.

"You see what greed has caused, Susan? Three people dead, you in jail . . . was it worth it?"

She didn't answer. She placed her head in her hands and sobbed.

Justin stared at her. She was broken. Any feelings he had for her seem to wash away with her tears. Some things were just not meant to be.

Susan looked up and met his stare, tears streaming down her cheeks. "I'm sorry, Justin. I didn't mean to hurt you."

"Yes, you did Susan. It was all in your grand plan." He turned and walked away.

Chapter Twenty

Justin joined two uniformed officers in the all night restaurant, sitting over coffee and donuts.

"You guys assigned to the beach tonight?" he asked.

"Yeah," one officer answered.

"Yeah, me too. I haven't done anything like this since I left the department up north. It brings back memories."

The younger officer looked fresh out of Officer Cadet training. Was he even shaving yet? This hour of the night and no five-o-clock shadow. Justin rubbed his own scratchy chin. Oh boy, rookies. God, was he ever that young?

"I understand you shot a guy tonight," Officer Baby-face said.

"Yeah, that brought back memories, too. But my self-defense training kicked right back in. They shot at me . . . both of them, so I had no choice."

The older officer nodded. "I don't mind firing on somebody that shoots back, but when I'm not 100% sure if they're armed, that troubles me."

"I've never shot anybody," Baby-face said. His face was ashen and he looked nervous, like he might puke.

"You'll be fine kid." Justin affirmed.
They sipped their coffees and Cherry Coke for Baby-face. Justin had seen this before. The silent nerves, where nobody talked, but everyone was psyching themselves up in their own way for the stake out.

"Just remember," Justin broke the silence. "That'll be me on the beach with a girl. So don't shoot me, okay?" The tension was broken and they laughed, walking out together.
The final briefing went smoothly. Justin chuckled when he counted twelve people assigned to the stake out, including him. *There's enough cops here to catch a stray fly.* Where was Sandy? She walked in wearing a skimpy bikini under a see-though cover-up walked into the briefing room. Didn't look so young and innocent now.

"We meet again," Justin smiled at her. "You know that we're supposed to act like lovers, don't you?"

Her eyes twinkled. "I'm looking forward to it."

Justin felt heat rise to his cheeks. What the hell? He didn't blush. "Well, now I am too. By the way," Justin said, "you hardly look like a cop in that . . . thing. Where do you hide your gun? Not that I'd want it any other way."

Sandy pointed to her beach bag, the handle of a revolver barely visible. She smiled and walked out ahead of Justin, pausing to ask which car was his.

"It's the one with the reclining seats," he said, with a broad smile.

They drove the short distance to the pier without speaking. The only thing that passed between them was an occasional glance. Sandy spread a blanket and lay her beach bag down, her gun covered in a towel just under the unzipped flap.

Justin lay down on his back, put his hands under his head and stared at the stars. "You know, Sandy, this could be a wonderful world if people weren't on it. We certainly can screw up things. Look how peaceful and beautiful the stars are."

She looked up at the stars and nodded, then turned to him. "We were given orders, Justin, and I never disobey an order." She leaned over and kissed him softly. His arms came up and encircled her, pulling her down to him. They kissed long and tenderly.

"You're a very pretty lady, Sandra, I think . . ." She pressed her fingers to his lips.

"Where did this Sandra come from? Everybody calls me Sandy."

"I like Sandra better. That is your name, isn't it?"

"Yes, that's my given name, but . . ." This time Justin stopped her in mid-sentence.

"Sandra sounds classier. Let your friends and the people you work with call you Sandy. I want to call you Sandra."

"You're an awful nice man, Justin." She leaned over and kissed him again. Their tongues found each other and the kiss lasted a long time before they separated.

She pulled away from him. Justin felt the cool breeze from the ocean cool his body where her warm body had just been. "You never knew it, Justin. But I used to watch you in the station when you came in to see Muldoon. I always thought there was something special about you."

"Why didn't I ever see you?"

She tucked her hair behind her ear. "Because I was a young rookie cop and never wanted you to see me staring at you."

"Maybe you should have. Maybe we could have been on this beach like this sooner."

"I'm pretty sure of it . . . now." Justin looked up at the pier. Where was this connection and where was Kegg? He knew the undercover guys were already in place, even if he couldn't see them. A car pulled up and parked next to the entrance of the pier.

"That must be the bait," Sandy said.

"Yeah, that's Kegg. Okay, Sandra, don't be nervous. Let them think were lovers. If they see us making noise they won't think we're watching them."

"You're a smart one, aren't you? Did you forget I'm an undercover agent?" She kissed him on the cheek.

He grinned. "Apparently not smart enough to have found you, until now."

"You're a charmer," she said, laughing out loud, the sound carrying across the water.

"That's it, make noise." He tickled her under her rib cage and she squirmed away, shrieking. "Come here, baby," he said loud enough for the benefit of anyone in ear shot.

Sandy nudged him. Another car had driven up, without its lights on. In the dim light, they could barely make out a man walking toward Kegg.

"You Kegg?"

Before he had a chance to answer, two undercover officers jumped from behind the bushes and had their guns in the man's ribcage before he knew what was happening. Justin and Sandy ran up the steps of the pier to see other officers surrounding the second car that drove up with all four doors wide open. Sergeant

Muldoon pulled the driver out of the car. He forced him over the hood while the other officers frisked him for weapons. They cuffed him and John spun him around to face him.

"What's your name," John asked him. He didn't answer.
Justin reached for one of the officers flashlights and shone it in his face.

"I know you. I've seen you in front of the County Commissioners. You're Yale Duke." John emptied the man's pockets, throwing everything on the hood of the car. He opened his wallet, pulled out a credit card that confirmed his identification.

"Yup, it's him. Sandy, you may have the honors. Read them both their rights."

"I haven't done anything," said. Duke. "I just came to meet with my brother." He nodded his chin toward Carl Kegg.

John shook his head. "So now Kegg is your brother? Sterling Berns is dead. Need I say more?"

Duke sputtered with indignation. "I don't know what you're talking about. I know important people. You can't do this to me!"

"Is that so? John turned to the two officers flanking Duke. "Take them to the station. Let Lieutenant Chambers list the chargers."

John slapped Justin on his bare back. "It's all over, Slick. You did good work. We have our killers."

"And what about the necklace and Susan?" Justin asked.

"I believe that's up to the insurance company. She's committed fraud by having it all along. They may want to press charges against her, although I doubt it would keep her locked up."

Chapter Twenty One

Justin arrived at the police station early, at the same time as Lieutenant Chambers. They walked into the station together, and directly to John's office.

"Good morning, Toody," Justin said.

"Morning, Slick."

Lieutenant Chambers shook his head and chuckled, "You guys are crazy."

"Yeah," John said. "We are."

"John, when you have a moment, see me in my office." Lieutenant Chambers walked to his office.

"What's the word on Prudential pressing charges against Susan?" Justin asked his friend.

"Her big-shot attorney got to them. Pretty impressive that anyone could intimidate the deep pockets of the insurance world. Unless they didn't want to be caught up in a dispute that could last for years. They are dropping the charges against her and, of course, dropping her as a customer."

"Wow, Susan got off easy. So I guess you're going to release her now?"

John nodded. "With Kegg behind bars for killing Berns and Duke being held for arraignment for the murder of Richard Gauvin, there's nothing to hold Susan on. It's still possible the DA will try to implicate her in the Gauvin murder, but unless we see an arrest warrant, she is free to go."

"Can I talk to her before you release her?"

John looked at him like he was crazy. "Even with a fine woman like Sandy around, you're still carrying a flame for that broad, aren't you?"

No, he told himself. He just needed some closure. He followed John to the holding cell, his mind caught up in a million thoughts rushing through his head. Yea, Sandra was terrific. What was he doing? Maybe it was just his pride from being duped, and dumped by such a beautiful woman. Yes, he'd move on, maybe a little slower with Sandra, but he had to close the vault on this one.

Susan stood when he entered the cell. John left the door open and quietly slipped away, giving Justin and Susan some privacy.

"Susan. Prudential is dropping the charges against you. Your lawyers are good."

She smiled meekly. "They are paid well. Does this mean I am free to go?"

Justin nodded. "John is filling out your release papers now." He hesitated. Even with her make-up worn away and dressed in county issued scrubs, she was still beautiful. "Susan, can I ask you something?"

She looked up at him, her blue eyes penetrating him. "Okay."

"Did you mean any of it? When we made love, laughing and joking with me at Toody and Dorothy's . . .

or the opposite, when you called me vile names and said it was all an act. Which was the truth, Susan?"

She looked down and picked at invisible lint on her police issued wardrobe. "The truth? Even I don't know anymore. It's true that my marriage to Sterling was distant, at best. His greed consumed him and eventually, it consumed me too. When I stepped into that ratty office of yours, I thought it would be so easy to pull a ruse over the insurance company . . . and you. But things went all wrong. Nobody was supposed to get killed. We were in over our heads with those Duke Brothers."

He had to ask. Why did he want to torture himself so? "And me, it was all an act with me, too?"

"Oh Justin. Why did you have to turn out to be such a nice guy? Yes, okay, I'll admit it. I did . . . do . . . have feelings for you. But I suppose it is too late for any of that now."

Justin thought about the difference between Susan and Sandra. Susan was far more exotic and worldly, while Sandra had an innocence about her, even while having the hard inner core to fight crime as an undercover cop. He nodded.

"Call me old-fashioned, but I prefer my ladies without police records and ulterior motives. I could never trust you, Susan."

"That damn necklace. I swear, it is cursed. Seems like everyone that owns it ends up dead sooner or later," Susan said.

Justin felt the corners of his mouth turn up in slight smile. "Maybe because it never really belonged to any of those owners. Good-bye Susan." He turned and walked out of the cell. He didn't wait to talk to John before he left. He needed to get out of there, get some fresh air. He left the building and slipped behind the wheel of his trusty El Dorado. His cell phone rang as he pulled out of the parking lot. He recognized John's cell number on his caller ID. He tapped the screen.

"I take it that was tough for you." John said without waiting for Justin to speak.

"Yea, kind of. I need to get her out of my head."

"Good. My house, tomorrow morning. Just FYI, I'm inviting Sandy too. She's tougher than she looks, but God knows, she's going to have her hands full with you."

Justin laughed. It felt good. "Thanks, Pal, I'll see you then."

Dorothy served a large breakfast outside on their lanai, chatting with Sandra the entire time. Justin was pleased that Dorothy and Sandra hit it off as well as they did. His mind drifted off about anther time when he brought Susan to meet Dorothy and her mother. How proud he was of his sophisticated lady. If he would have been wiser, he would have seen through Susan's disguise. Was he seeing Sandra for who she really was? With a cop's salary, she sure wasn't flaunting anything. She seems grounded, sure of herself and what she wanted out of life. What did she want? An old P.I. like himself? This time, he would take his time, give himself . . . and Sandra, time to learn about each other, perhaps to fall in love the right way.

Acknowledgements

I want to thank Dr. Camisa of Naples Florida for his important medical input where and when needed. Thank you, doctor.

I want to thank my editor, Joanne Tailele for spending many hours editing this book. Her expertise and telephone calls between us was much more than either of us anticipated. I thought it was ready for print, but it was her that made it possible. I can't thank her enough!

And, to my wife, Rochelle who put up with my time spent typing away for so many hours.

To my many readers who have either purchased this book, either as a print edition or as an e-book.

And to my two wonderful kids, Susan and Wade, who thinks their dad is quite a guy.

I hope you all enjoyed all of my novels. I'd appreciate your feedback. I can be emailed at: dansbooks@embarqmail.com